Them Summer Daze

DOROTHY GIVENS TERRY

ISBN: 979-8-218-27331-6

Cover design: By the author

Many thanks to the loving family and encouraging friends who supported my efforts in making this work possible.

CONTENTS

What to know before you go…

Welcome to Charleston, South Carolina, circa 1969!

Before you journey through this crazy summer, check out the map on the next page to get the lay of the neighborhood.

Also, some words used throughout this story reflect local and regional dialect, so check out the glossary in the back to find out what words like *boonkey, ninny* or *nanny* mean. Can you guess?

TV shows that are mentioned throughout the book are explained in the glossary, as well as local landmarks, famous people, and pivotal local and national events of that time.

Also, songs that were hits between January and August of 1969 are reflected in the chapter headings (see the Table of Contents) and others within the chapters themselves. You'll find the names of the artists in the glossary as well. Can you guess some of them?

Lastly, there are a lot of names in this story of the people who populated the neighborhood in this little corner of the world. You don't have to remember most of them. Just keep your eyes on the main character throughout the story, and you'll be fine. That's it! You're now ready to experience *Them Summer Daze!*

The Lay of the Neighborhood

Past is Prologue

I was born with a *caul* over my face. I had to look that word up when I was old enough to wonder what a caul was and after I heard the story of how I was born, over and over again, mostly from my grandmother.

A caul is like a thin veil that covers a baby's face at birth. This is extremely rare, so I was told. And some people attach all kinds of meaning to it. My grandmother told me that being born like this means I have the second sight, the third eye – that I can see the future. She called this a gift, but I considered it a nuisance. Because, you know what? I did "see" stuff, sometimes.

By that I mean, images would float up in my head, like those "predictions" in a *Magic Eight Ball.* Something that seemed random, like a dog that I'd never seen before. And then, a few days later, that exact same dog would wander into the yard – a stray, lost and seeming to belong to no one.

Sounds cool, right? But the thing about these images is they're not connected to anything, so I don't know what they mean at the time. Take the dog, for example. I didn't know that I'd see that dog wandering into our yard a few days later. But that same dog could have just as well walked up to me, and bit me on the leg. Who knew? I certainly didn't, which is why I considered these images a nuisance.

So what, I could kinda see stuff before it happened. It didn't mean that I could stop anything from happening. I did get a queasy kind of feeling and goosebumps when the image in my head connected with something happening in real life – like when the dog just wandered into the yard. "There it is," I thought.

Random images didn't float around in my head very often, thank goodness. And I wasn't supposed to talk about it, anyway. Mama thought that talk of visions and images were some old-timey, slavery days, voodoo hoodoo junk that Grandmama liked to keep going, on account of her reputation as the neighborhood *root woman.*

I didn't have to look up that word – "root" – to know what it meant when it was used to describe Grandmama, because as long as I could remember, she was considered the go-to person to fix whatever ailed you. Not like a doctor, but more on that later.

Anyway, I think Mama was embarrassed by Grandmama and her root ways, and I think my "visions" scared her too. When I was younger, I'd tell Mama about the images when they popped up. But as I got older, I recognized that look of fear on Mama's face when I'd bring it up. At first, she'd brush my visions aside. Then, she just told me to keep them to myself, unless of course, I saw something that involved life or death. But like I said, I didn't know what the images meant at the time I saw them, so how would I know if they were connected to life-or-death situations?

Daddy wasn't freaked out by my visions, though. He would

always (half-jokingly) ask me to "see" some digits so that he could win at *the numbers*. I'd spit out some random numbers, just so that he would leave me alone; although I knew my visions didn't work that way.

Like I said, I didn't see these images that often. But, during the summer of 1969, my visions seemed to have gone into overdrive. Here I was, expecting another hot, muggy, buggy Charleston summer, with nothing much to do except baby sit the twins; go to my best friend Antoinette's birthday party; hang out with my cousins *from off*, when the New York City relatives came to visit; and attend the subsequent all-day-and-well-into-the-night annual family gathering, usually at Riverside Beach.

I'd have plenty of time left over to do what I really had planned for my summer – conquering the art of "cool." Yep, by the time I busted through the doors of Buist School for my last year of middle school in the fall, I was going to be transformed into the icon of cool. From head to toe: hair, clothes and attitude, I'd be just like the *Project Girls.*

Aaaah, the Project Girls. Lisa, Sherry, and Rosemarie. Now, those girls oozed cool. Even their names were cool, and not the hokey Dorothy/Dottie that everyone called me.

The Project Girls knew how to dance (even if Mama thought they danced too *loose*). They knew how to dress (even if Mama thought they dressed too *grown*). They had cool hair – Lisa with the sky-high Afro, Rosemarie with the permed, slicked-down boy cut like Mia Farrow in *"Rosemary's Baby,"* and Sherry, who was mixed with something, with the long, dark, wavy "Indian" hair that she usually wore in two thick, ninny-scraping braids.

Oh, and that's the other cool thing about them – they all have ninnies, and there I was, ninny-less, and period-less, and almost thirteen!

Well, I couldn't rush Mother Nature, but while I was waiting to, uh, bloom – I was going to make good use of my time. Armed with a notebook, I was going to spend the summer doing "Cool Case Studies." (Is keeping a notebook on how to be cool, "cool?")

Well, Mama always said that I had more book sense than common sense, so maybe doing observations like we did in science class was the way to go! Wish I could put those Project Girls under a microscope!

Anyway, that was the plan for the summer, but what is that saying about the best-laid plans? Because, while my Grandmama thought I had "the vision" and could see the future, I was definitely looking the wrong way when I got blindsided by the summer of 1969!

THEM SUMMER DAZE

THEM SUMMER DAZE

JUNE

Out of School

THEM SUMMER DAZE

1 CAN'T GET NEXT TO YOU

So, I had a "vision" earlier today.

I was in the bathroom, trying to get my hair in two Afro puffs like the "Beauty of the Week" lady in one of the stacks of *JET* magazines Mama had around the house.

I thought I'd start my "Quest for Cool" by changing my hair from the nanny-roller braids I'd been wearing since first grade, into something more up to date.

Easy enough but getting a straight part down the middle of my head was giving me the fits. And while I was trying to look at the back of my head in the mirror over the sink, by standing on the edge of the tub, I had a vision of a pickle bouncing along on the sidewalk. Like I said, I don't know what my visions mean, but something involving a bouncing pickle was going to happen sooner or later.

Maybe it just meant that I would buy a pickle from the store once Mama got home from the laundromat and gave me any extra quarters she had for my babysitting the twins. To be honest, I wasn't really watching them; I just made them jelly bread, and plunked them down in front of the TV, where they would be mesmerized by their favorite show, *Star Trek*, at least for a half hour. But the half hour must be up because I was hearing that soaring ending theme music — ♪Do-OOOOH! Ooh-ooh-ooh-ooh-OOH! ♪

I jumped down off the edge of the tub, ran into the kitchen, and flipped through the three channels, looking for another show for them to watch. The public TV channel was the fourth channel, but it didn't always come in clear. I flipped to it anyway. A children's show called June Bug was on. The picture came in kind of fuzzy, but they wanted to watch it anyway, fascinated that they were watching a channel coming in all the way from Columbia, the state capital.

"I'll be in the living room; don't touch the TV, and don't go out the kitchen door."

"Oh, you not supposed to be in the living room," they both kind of chimed, almost in unison.

"Peter and Paul, shut up!" I snapped back.

Everybody thought the twins were "too cute," and I used to think so too, when they were younger. When people who didn't know us would stop us in the street to admire the twins' cuteness, and ask their names, upon hearing "Peter and Paul," they would ask me: "So is your name Mary?" They'd chuckle before I could say "no," thinking they were being clever, but I heard that question a million times before, and it stopped being funny a long time ago. They would walk off, still chuckling, before I could explain that my daddy's name was Paul, and his granddaddy, my great granddaddy, was named Peter. The twins that everybody thought were so cute, were now six-year-old terrors headed to first grade at the same school as me in the fall. (The elementary and middle school were in the same building, which was why I couldn't be leaving Buist School soon enough!)

But they were right, though. The living room was forbidden

territory, and I knew it. But it was the only room besides Mama and Daddy's bedroom – the other forbidden territory – that had an air conditioner in the window, which made sitting on the plastic-covered furniture all the more tolerable. Besides, I thought, 12-years old was old enough to be trusted to sit in a living room without making a mess.

I tossed some books (that needed to go back to the library because the due date was tomorrow) and a notepad on the coffee table next to a tarnishing tea set that was never used; I plunked myself down on the plastic-covered, hunter-green armchair, and plopped my bare feet up on the matching ottoman, also plastic covered, which matched the plastic-covered sofa, and the plastic-covered love seat. Even the lamps were still in the protective plastic that they came in from the store.

I was hoping to take the books back to the library today, except the library closed a half hour ago, at 5 p.m. And Mama still wasn't back from the laundromat, which was starting to be a cause for concern. I could catch the library tomorrow, but all the neighborhood corner stores closed at 6 p.m., and after that bouncing pickle vision, I was really wanting a sour dill.

The short-gloved hand on my Cinderella watch that I got for Christmas, pointed to the five. The long-gloved hand pointed to the six. Thirty more minutes to go. (Is a Cinderella watch cool?) Might as well make use of the time:

"Cool" Case Study #1

June 6, 1969

I hereby pledge to transform myself into a Cool Girl by the time I return for the 8th grade this fall at Buist School. I will accomplish this goal by doing the following:

Cool	**Not Cool**
Change my hair: Wear an Afro or Afro puffs or Cornrows (Will Mama let me get a straight perm?)	*Nanny-roller* plaits or Shirley Temple press and curl
Learn how to dance (like the Project Girls)	I hope the school is done with teaching us how to square dance! (Although I did like the bamboo dance)
Update my wardrobe (to look more like the Project Girls) By wearing: Halter tops Midi tops Smock tops Tennis shoes Buffalo sandals Hercules sandals Any kind of sandals Clogs	Dresses of any kind (except maybe a maxi) Blouses with Peter Pan collars Loafers Patent leather shoes
Grow some ninnies! (like the Project Girls)	How did theirs grow out before mine? We're all the same age! (And I'm period-less, too!!! Maybe that's why I don't have any ninnies!)

2 BABY, BABY, DON'T CRY

My world was bound by Reid Street to the north, Calhoun Street to the south, East Bay Street to the east and Meeting Street to the west.

A teacher once told my class that the streets in between – Mary, Ann, Judith, John, Alexander, Charlotte, Henrietta and the street I lived on, Elizabeth – were named after the children of some long-ago neighborhood landowner.

The long-ago landowner's name was Mister Joseph Mazyck. I knew some Mazycks from school, but they were black like me, and the long-ago landowner was white. No relation, I suppose, but you never know.

In a not very big town, sometimes called the Holy City for its seeming overabundance of churches, my little neighborhood had its share – five – and an equal number of corner stores. I had about 10 minutes to catch one of those stores open, after Mama finally came home, catching me with my blouse up and tucked under my chin, while I looked down at my very flat chest, searching for a sign, ANY sign, that I was about to bloom out at any minute. Nothing!

"Girl, what you doing? Put your blouse down and help me with this laundry basket!"

Hearing Mama's voice, the twins rushed into the living room.

"Mama, she been in here the whole time," said one.

"With her foot up on the little chair," said the other one.

I shoved each tattletale twin, to shush them.

"Stop pushing your brothers. I know you weren't sitting up in my living room after I done told y'all to stay out."

"No'm," I mumbled.

"Oh, she *telling a story*!"

Another shove, one for each boy.

"Would y'all stop! Girl, help me with this basket!"

I helped Mama lift the two-wheeled laundry basket into the living room.

"Mama, you promised me the quarters…"

Mama cut me off.

"I shouldn't give you anything if you can't watch these *chirren* right. And what do you need to buy from the store? Y'all got all those *chilly bears* in the freezer no one's eating."

I stood silent. She was right. There were six frozen paper cups of cherry Kool-Aid in the freezer, but I wanted something different. Besides, I thought I was getting too old to eat chilly bears.

"Here!" Mama reached into the front of her dress and pulled out a red plastic change purse. She squeezed it open and dumped four quarters into my waiting palm.

"Hurry back so you can help me fold this laundry!"

"Bring us something back!" one of the twins yelled at my rapidly retreating back.

"You wish!"

I passed the closed door of *Miss Smith's* store on the bottom floor of her house at the corner of Charlotte and Elizabeth streets. I couldn't remember the last time her store had been open. All her stuff was stale anyway. Every kid and adult in the neighborhood agreed that Miss Smith had really gotten too old to be running a business. Her store smelled musty, her inventory was dusty and her eyesight was so bad, she could barely see the mice running about the place.

Miss Smith was one of the last white people left in the neighborhood and she was the one oldest person that most of us knew, so she was a bit of a novelty. We'd go in there just to poke around and to look at her head of fluffy white hair. Some of the more daring kids would try to confuse her, while the other kids helped themselves to the outdated items on her shelves. Miss Smith just stood behind the counter, absent-mindedly smiling. Stealing is a sin, but the thieves rationalized that in this case, it's not really, since Miss Smith's stuff was so stale, they were actually doing her a favor by taking it off her hands, or rather, off her shelves.

I hurried on past the Smith store, crossed Charlotte Street and passed the high brick wall, behind which was the graveyard of the Second Presbyterian Church.

Maybe I can catch Mister Henry's store at the corner of Elizabeth and John streets. A tall, rail thin, cranky old Bahamian man, Mister Henry had a very neat store, unlike Miss Smith's, and he never seemed to tire of telling us that he plans to keep it that way.

"What you want?" He would bark as soon as we entered. "You bahd chirren better not come in heah messing up my stoh!"

Since his cookies were always so fresh, it was worth getting cussed out by him just to buy five cents worth of the ginger snaps or the sandwich crèmes in lemon or strawberry or vanilla or the shortbreads or the lemon wafers or the lady fingers, all on display in giant see-through plastic canisters, topped with silver lids and lined up along the counter.

But darn! He was closed too.

There was the old German, Mister Grundgen over on Charlotte and Alexander. Sometimes, he forgot to close at 6 o'clock. Maybe if I hurried…

But…

I heard the train coming down John Street, its whistle hooting, and wheels click clacking, as it chugged toward me on tracks that sliced through the city from the *North Area* and headed to the docks just beyond East Bay Street.

At 12-years old, I was probably getting a little too old for this, but I just couldn't resist.

I pressed my back against the wooden side of Mister Henry's store anyway and waited.

Normally, I'd run out and put a penny on the track so the train could flatten it under its wheels of steel as it chugged on by. I would run out onto the tracks after the train had passed, and hold the hot, smooth coin in my hand. But all I had were the quarters and I darn sure wasn't going to part with any of those.

Here it comes!

I pressed harder into the wall as the train thundered by, the box cars swaying slightly as the train made its way down to the docks. The air was whipped up around me, enough to make my newly created Afro puffs dance in the breeze. A box car or two had been known to derail – rare, but it has happened a few times, skidding off the tracks with a piercing shriek and crashing to the street with a loud thud that could be heard for blocks.

I was separated from this calamity only by the sidewalk, which was not very wide and which was rumbling under my feet, and a little square of grass between the sidewalk and the curb.

The thought of a box car possibly derailing and careening toward me, both frightened and excited me. Will I be able to run to safety at the first sign of trouble? My knees shook as I stood on my little shaky square of sidewalk. My back was literally up against the wall; I was trapped; I was paralyzed. Will this train ever end? Will it end up on me?

I was saved from this possible calamity by a hand grabbing my arm and dragging me to safety.

"Nette! You scared the stuffing out of me! I thought you was Dugga!"

The train thundered on by, but my heart was still pounding.

"Girl, old Dugga don't hang out round here. You gotta go down the tracks behind the warehouses on East Bay Street if you wanna do the *nasty* with him."

Nette was my sometimes best friend. Sometimes, because she got on my nerves when she did stuff like grab my arm and scare me half to death like that, and she was always talking about the nasty.

Nette was short for Antoinette, who was laughing at me as I said, "Nobody wants to do anything with the likes of creepy Dugga. I just thought… Oh, never mind! Come on!"

"Where we going?"

"To catch Mister Grundgen's store open. I got four quarter, and I might buy you something, if you stop laughing and stop talking about that *fresh* Dugga AND stop talking about the nasty."

"OK."

We rushed back down Elizabeth Street and hung a left past Ebenezer Church onto Charlotte Street, passing Nette's humongous two-story, two-porch, white house across the street. Nette has the reputation of being the richest black girl that any of us knew. But you couldn't tell from the way she acted, which was not snotty or snobby – the way you would think a girl who lived in a big house like that would act, which is why I liked her.

I could see Mister Grundgen's store on the next corner at Charlotte and Alexander. And the lights were on! Maybe if we hurry…

But…those double stairwells were beckoning.

We were probably getting a little too old for this, but without saying a word, Nette and I approached a house, quickly charged up one side of a set of semi-circular stairs and arrived breathlessly on a small landing. We took turns ringing the doorbell, ran down an identical set of stairs on the other side of the landing and back onto the sidewalk.

We'd be halfway down the street by the time an old white lady, whose face was so puckered and wrinkled and scary, that we called her a real-life witch, came to the door, hunched over a cane and draped in clothes that looked like the last century.

She, like Miss Smith, was a remnant of what this neighborhood must have looked like in the days of Mister Joseph Mazyck. Marooned in their big, falling-down, old houses, they were an ever-shrinking island of whiteness in an ocean of black families, left to suffer the indignities of the children of those black families.

"Pickaninnies!" The real-life witch hissed at our retreating backs, as we ran laughing down the street toward Mister Grundgen's store.

When we arrived at the door, the lights were still on, the paper sign hanging in the door read, "Yes, we are open," but when we pushed the door, it was locked.

But there was Mister Grundgen, sitting on a stool behind his counter, wearing that dirty apron streaked with the dried blood of meat long-since sold.

Mister Grundgen had a temper even worse than Mister Henry's. But at least Mister Henry put on a smile for the adult customers. Mister Grundgen wouldn't even try that. He always seemed to be in a bad mood and acted like he'd rather set fire to the store with us in it, than sell us anything, including a bar of that scratchy *Octagon* soap that Mama sent us here to get sometimes.

Mister Grundgen didn't have much in his store anyway, at least not anything that a kid would really like; just some weird-looking meats, cans of beer with weird-sounding names, a small variety of chips, pretzels and candy, and that's about it.

Daddy said that Mister Grundgen is nasty and blows his nose in his apron and we shouldn't buy anything from him anyway, especially meat, even if he's slightly cheaper than the *Piggly Wiggly* over on Meeting Street or *GEX*, a store *up the road.*

Because of his accent, the boys in the neighborhood have built up this whole story around Mister Grundgen being some kind of Nazi war criminal hiding out in the United States, goose stepping around his store after hours yelling, "Achtung!" like the soldiers in *Hogan's Heroes.*

Who knows and who cares! He didn't look like some war criminal right at that moment though, just a grumpy old man slumped over asleep on a stool behind the counter in his dingy-looking store.

We banged on the glass, which stirred Mister Grundgen awake. He scowled at us, rose from the stool, marched to the door and flipped the sign to: "Sorry, we are closed!" He turned off the lights and marched through a door at the back of the now darkened store. You know, marching around like that, he did look like a German soldier. Achtung, indeed!

Oh well, two more stores to go.

Without saying a word to each other, Nette and I bolted down Alexander Street, cut through Cedar Court, and back onto Elizabeth Street, which would put us past the adults who were probably gathering right about now for their evening sit down on the bench in the yard, in front of the four-apartment house where I lived.

I was supposed to stay out of Cedar Court, which was on a long list of places I wasn't supposed to be, things I wasn't supposed to do and people I wasn't supposed to hang out with. Mama never told me why I should stay out of there, except to note that the people living in the run-down houses along what was really an alley, seemed a little worse for wear than the people living on the other streets in our neighborhood. Whatever.

But I didn't want to run the risk of seeing Mama sitting on the bench. She would probably stop me in my tracks and end my corner-store crusade.

Nette and I popped out of the other end of Cedar Court, without incident, and arrived at Mister Bongi's now closed store. This was a shame, because Mister Bongi had the best pickled everything: pig's feet, eggs, hot sausages, peppers and of course – just plain old pickles. Mister Bongi acts like he doesn't want us in his store either, never mind that the place always smelled like kerosene. Mama didn't like us going there anyway, because she said that Mister Bongi had no shame in opening on Sunday, flouting both God and the *Blue Laws*.

We thought that Mister Bongi was black, but Mama said he was Indian, although he looked nothing like the Indians we saw on the TV westerns my brothers were always watching, like *Gunsmoke* or *Bonanza.* "He's from India," Mama explained. Oh. That must account for his *"good"* but graying hair.

Well, on to the last stop – Costa's.

Sitting catty-corner at Elizabeth and Calhoun streets, and the southern boundary to my 12-year-old world, Constantopoulos (as the sign stated in big, black block letters above the door), was the last corner store in the neighborhood. This was it!

As we rushed across Elizabeth Street, out of the corner of my eye, I saw Donnalee – who was about our age – upstairs on the porch of her house, which sat at the edge of Cedar Court, looking toward Costa's store.

"If you see my mama in Mister Costa, tell her I'm waitin'," she yelled.

Costa was really one of the best corner stores in the city – a stand-alone cinder block building painted Barbados pink on the outside, with clean linoleum floors and stuff on shelves along short aisles inside, almost like a real grocery store. Costa's was a big step up from the other musty-smelling stores in the neighborhood with their creaky, rundown wood floors, operating out of what used to be the front room of some old Charleston house.

Nobody really knew where Mister Costa came from, but rumor among the grown-ups, who talked about a lot of stuff at the bench when they thought we weren't listening, was that he jumped ship when a Greek tanker he was working on docked in the Charleston Harbor. When the tanker pulled out, he was left behind.

Even though the name posted up over the door read Constantopoulos, nobody in the neighborhood could pronounce it, so we promptly shortened his name to just "Costa." Mister Costa was a short man with a big head topped with very thick and very dark hair and didn't seem to mind the name change. A man of few words, he sat quietly on a stool behind the counter with his big hairy arms folded, smiling as we tramped up and down the aisles, looking at everything before we spent our nickel, dime or quarter.

Even if we didn't have money, he'd let us get stuff on credit up to a dollar, not questioning us as we lied and said our mama told us to put the items on her account. He'd just smile and scoop up the penny candies like Mary Janes and Squirrel Nuts and Kits, with his big hairy hands, and tossed them into a little brown paper bag. Or he'd hand us a pack of Now and Laters, a Sour Pop, Sweet Tarts, Pixie Stix, or a box of Mike and Ikes, Red Hots or Lemon Heads. Sometimes, without our asking, he'd throw in bubble gum cigarettes, or candy lipsticks, wax soda bottles filled with sweet juice or candy necklaces, bracelets and candy buttons spread out in pastel dots on white sheets of paper. And, if the Lance cookies or Rock 'n Rolls were getting a little stale, he'd just give them away too.

I felt proud to have my own dollar on that day, thank you! But I wouldn't be spending at Costa's, either, because he was closed, too!

We were just in time to see Mister Costa usher Miss Frannie, Donnalee's mother, with a hand placed at the small of her back, through a door that led to the storage area at the back of the now darkened store.

So that was that. All the corner stores were closed. No sour pickle; no red-hot potato chips; no cookies; no candy.

We headed back down Elizabeth Street toward home, walking slowly. Across the street, I saw Donnalee, still leaning over the upstairs porch, waiting for her mother.

"You see my mama at Mister Costa's?" She shouted down at us as we walked by on the other side of the street.

Well yes and no. "Mister Costa's closed," I offered, not knowing if I should say more.

"But we saw her. She'll be out soon," Nette hollered up to her. "As soon as she finishes doing the nasty with Mister Costa," she whispered to me.

"Nette!"

Why did she always have to talk about the nasty? But that *was* a rumor swirling about the neighborhood, spoken in whispers among the adults. Miss Frannie may have been the reason that Mister Costa never got back on that tanker for the return trip to Greece.

"We…can…go…to…the Nugget," Nette said slowly as we dragged down the street.

I stopped on the sidewalk.

The Nugget was on that list of places that I was not supposed to go, and Nette knew that. She knew she shouldn't go there either. The Nugget, on the next corner on the same side of the street as Costa's, was the corner store of last resort – so named because it was open until the wee hours, and it did have some corner store stuff, like potato chips, bags of nuts, chewing gum and pickled stuff in glass jars.

But the Nugget was a straight-up bar, complete with a neon OPEN sign flashing in the window. The window's centerpiece and a source of mesmerizing entertainment for the neighborhood kids since it was installed earlier this year, was a neon bottle with little sparkly lights that are supposed to be champagne bubbles that change from red to yellow to blue to green as the bottle "filled" to the top. Once filled, the neon bottle "tipped" and the electric bubbles would pour out and rapidly dissipate, one by one. The bottle righted itself, and then filled up with electric bubbles all over again.

It's not like I haven't been in the Nugget before. Last spring, when Mama wanted some stuff from Piggly Wiggly and was afraid Daddy would get home after the store closed, she sent me into the Nugget with a list of stuff for him to get before he came home, like Karo syrup, Carnation Instant Milk, *BC Powder*, *Kotex*, and some other boring stuff.

I remember pushing through the heavy wooden door and being immediately enveloped in darkness and smoke, with music blaring from a jukebox somewhere. I stood in the darkness waiting for my eyes to adjust to the light when: "What you doing in here, girl?" A voice from the darkness.

Daddy. But because I couldn't see very well, not even in the daylight, much less a dark bar, I froze at the door and squinted through the darkness trying to locate Daddy among the shapes hunched on stools at a counter or the other shapes sitting at one of the few tables and chairs outlining a small dance floor. Was he going to make me stumble around in here, trying to find him?

Before I could figure out what to do, Daddy materialized from the murkiness. I was relieved! Without a word, I handed him the list, which he read quickly and crumpled into the pocket of his work shirt.

"Tell your mama okay and tell her don't send you in here no more."

Fine with me. Still without a word, I turned and tugged at the handle on the wooden door, then hurried back out into the daylight, trailing the scent of cigarette smoke and beer behind me.

With that uncomfortable memory on my mind, I said to Nette, "What if my daddy's in there? I've told you I'm not supposed to go in there."

"We can look around for his car," Nette answered. "Or give me the money. I go in there all the time. I'll get the stuff." She was lying. She did not go in the Nugget all the time. The owner, Mister Knox, ran kids out all the time, but sometimes allowed the teenagers to come in and buy stuff.

We arrived at the door of the bar. I gave Nette two quarters and she reached for the handle on the wooden door.

"Wait!" I wasn't sure that I trusted Nette with my money.

I surveyed the street. I didn't see Daddy's light blue Buick.

We went through the wooden door.

Nette, not bothered by the smoke, loud music or darkness, grabbed me by the hand and pranced up to the bar like she *did* come in here a lot.

"Two bags of red-hot potato chips and two sour dill pickles, please!" she ordered.

I froze.

There at the bar was Daddy, his back turned to me and his hand resting at the small of the back of a woman in a very tight jumpsuit, like the way Mister Costa had his hand at Miss Frannie's back as he led her through the back-room door of his store.

"Two bags of red-hot chips and two pickles, PLEASE!" Nette got louder at the indignity of not being heard the first time.

The loud voice got the attention of the bar patrons, including the jumpsuit lady and my daddy. They all turned to regard the impudent child.

The jumpsuit lady's eyes traveled from Nette to me. She was wearing lots of eye shadow, lots of bangles on her wrists, huge hoop earrings and an Afro that would make *Angela Davis* jealous. She was pretty.

"Oh, look," she said, "Looks like someone has sent her little spy to spy on you, Paul!" Some of the bar crowd laughed. Daddy's hand fell away from the small of the jumpsuit lady's back. The seconds seemed to drag out into slow-motion minutes before he finally said, "I thought I told you not to come in here. Go home."

My face got hot, and my ability to move returned as I spun on my heels, yanked at the wooden door and was back out on the sidewalk, where I took in big gulps of the hot evening air.

I was shaking. I thought I was going to cry. I didn't know why and I didn't want to cry. Nette came back out a few minutes later.

"Hey, what happened to you? I turned around and you were gone! Here's your pickle. I got one, too." The pickles were wrapped in wax paper.

"I don't want it anymore. I've lost my taste for it." I snatched one of the wax-paper wrapped pickles from her hand and threw it to the ground. The pickle escaped its wrapping and did little bounces along the sidewalk before it rolled off the curb and landed in the gutter.

Then came the goosebumps and that queasy feeling when my visions crashed into reality. There it is! The bouncing pickle from the vision I had earlier today.

I left Antoinette and the pickle on the street and hurried home.

◆◆◆

"Mama?"

"Hmmm?"

"You ever think about getting an Afro?"

We were folding the laundry on the bed in her bedroom.

After leaving Nette and my pickle on the sidewalk, I ran home, glancing over at the bench, as I turned into the yard, relieved that Mama wasn't sitting out there, swatting away mosquitoes in the fading sunlight like the other ladies.

I snatched my notebook from the sofa, where I had left it for just anybody to see and almost made it to my room before Mama stopped me in my tracks.

"Come and help me fold this laundry."

I tossed the notebook behind a low bookcase in the hallway on my way into Mama's room. I could hear the twins splashing around in the tub.

Mama looked up at me briefly but didn't ask what I got from the store or why I didn't get anything from the store, and I didn't offer up any explanations.

"What would I want with all that nappy hair piled up on top of my head?" She answered my question about her getting an Afro, while quickly folding clothes. "Looks like a bug catcher, that's what it looks like to me."

"Oh. I dunno. It could be…cool, I guess." Mama had already had her head scarf on for the night, after setting her hair on makeshift rollers fashioned from brown paper bags.

"Cool?" Mama sniffed. "Well, don't you go thinkin' I'mma let you get one. Those giant puffs are about as far as you going with that mess." Mama nodded with disdain at my new hairdo.

I had forgotten about my experiment in Afro puffs. I self-consciously patted my hair.

We continued to fold clothes in silence. I tried not to think about the jumpsuit lady. How come I didn't have *that* vision, instead of some stupid bouncing pickle that didn't warn me of anything! See what I mean about my visions? Useless!

"This is a man's world. This is a maaaaan's world!"

I was awakened by a late-night James Brown impersonator in the kitchen.

After folding the laundry with Mama, I shooed the twins out of the bathroom and hurried through my own bath, not wanting to run into Daddy before I went to bed. I wanted to take a shower because it was quicker, but Mama believed that only men take showers, not women, girls or children. And besides, she didn't want me to wet up my hair.

By the time I got out of the bath, the twins had fallen asleep in the bunk beds across the room from my own bed. It sucked sharing a room with my little brothers, but there was no other place to sleep. I had asked to sleep in the living room on the sofa, which pulled out into a bed. But Mama thought that young girls shouldn't "sleep out," whatever that meant. Mama was full of rules for young girls.

"This is a man's world. This is a maaaaan's world!"

The singing continued, then a pause.

Pot tops were being lifted and slammed back down.

"This isssss a maaaaaaaaaan's world! A man's WORLD!"

Another pause.

The refrigerator door was opened and slammed shut.

"This is a man's world. This is a man's world." Daddy never gets past that line in the song.

My stomach was in knots. I'd fallen asleep with my notebook that I'd retrieved from behind the bookcase before I went to bed and now the spiraled wire binding was digging into my cheek. But I dared not move, less he heard my bed creak.

Would he come back here and yell at me for being in the Nugget earlier? Would I get my *boonkey* cut, even though I was getting too old for a whipping? Would he put me on punishment, making me miss Nette's upcoming birthday party?

The door to the other bedroom was opened and slammed shut.

"Hey!" Daddy yelled from the kitchen.

The bathroom door was opened and slammed shut: It was Mama.

Now I had to use the bathroom too!

The bathroom door was opened and slammed shut again. And then the bedroom door, again.

Another "hey" from Daddy, but Mama was apparently ignoring him.

Then the bedroom door was opened and slammed shut, again.

Muffled voices, getting louder. And louder.

Angry words seeped through the walls.

"Shouldn't be in there!"

"Got something to hide?"

I was frozen in place. The notebook was really digging into my cheek. But I couldn't move. I had caused this.

My brothers slept hard. They didn't move.

A siren wailed in the distance. Did someone call the police on our little family drama?

The bedroom door was opened and slammed shut, again. I heard Daddy in the living room and the creak of the sofa bed being pulled out.

After what seemed like forever, snoring.

Was it safe to go to the bathroom now? Because now, I *really* had to go! I eased out of bed, notebook in hand and crept toward the bathroom. Silence from the other bedroom. Snoring getting louder and louder in the living room. Daddy left the kitchen light on. I turned it off.

<u>"Cool" Case Study #2</u>

Cool	Not Cool
Mr. Costa and his store (when he's open!)	The Nugget — The Corner Store of Last Resort (especially when your dad catches you in there)
Having a best friend, like Nette	Having a best friend who talks too much about the nasty!
Having four quarters	Having no place to spend four quarters
Lots of bangles	Lots of bangles on a lady your daddy has his arms around
Knowing stuff grown-ups don't think you know (like whatever's happening in the back of that store with Mr. Costa and Miss Frannie	Knowing stuff grown-ups don't think you know (like whatever's happening with Daddy and the lady at the bar
The Project Girls	Having a daddy around, unlike The Project Girls

3 RUNAWAY CHILD, RUNNING WILD

I awoke to a quiet house. Peter was snoring lightly. Paul had a pillow over his head. Was he dead?

I always slept wearing my Cinderella watch. Cinderella's shorter arm pointed to the eight. The long arm pointed to twelve.

I was hungry and I had to go to the bathroom. I wanted to get out of this bedroom that was already starting to steam up from the summer heat, even though it was still morning and all the windows were wide open to let in any breeze that decided to blow my way.

Did I dream last night?

I listened hard, trying to hear if any sound was coming from the other bedroom. Nothing. Any more snoring from the living room? Nothing. I eased out of bed and shucked off an old *slip* that I slept in as pajamas and quickly dressed into a pair of shorts and a top.

Will I ever have my own room? I opened the closet and faced the makeshift toy box in front of me, which was really just a big cardboard box that I, and some of the neighborhood kids, had dragged all the way from the back of Robinson Bicycle Shop over on King Street.

The box was starting to cave in on its front side, with toys from Christmases past threatening to avalanche onto the bedroom floor. To one side of the box was a pile of shoes. Shoes from Easter, church shoes, old school shoes, *draggers*. And my tan-colored Keds.

My plan was to eat some cereal real quick in the kitchen, grab my library books off of the coffee table in the living room and ease out of the door to the library before anybody woke up.

But as I tip-toed my way to the bathroom, I could see Mama was already at the table, studying a cup of coffee.

"Going somewhere?" Mama asked without looking up.

"Um. Good morning. I need to take my books back to the library and I thought I'd hang out at Nette's…"

My voice trailed off.

"The library doesn't open for another hour, and it's too early to be visiting. Besides, I thought we'd go to King Street. I need to get some things and don't you need to get Antoinette a birthday present? You can drop your books off on the way and you can go see Antoinette after we get back."

"Yes, ma'am," I mumbled on the way to the bathroom. Normally, I'd be excited about a trip to King Street, but the thought of spending a few hours with Mama and having to talk about why I was in the Nugget yesterday and what I saw...!

"I'm gonna get the twins together and take 'em next door to Milly's." Mama rose from the table and dumped the rest of her coffee into the sink. "Be ready when I'm ready to go and make sure you comb that hair."

Mama rolled her eyes up at my mashed-down Afro puffs.

While I was in the living room gathering up my library books, I heard a lot of voices coming from the bench. With the adults either at work or sleeping off the night shift, the kids took over the bench during the day, but it seemed kind of early for even that.

I eased out the front door and hurried over to the commotion.

Everyone was crowded around three older boys, who had just pulled a huge box of toys into the yard.

Excited voices talking over each other.

"Where y'all get all this stuff?"

"Y'all stealing?"

"I'mma tell!"

"What happened?" I asked, squeezing my way into the group and staring down into the box.

"Robinson Bicycle Shop caught fire late last night," said one of the older boys.

Was that the siren that I heard over Mama and Daddy's raised voices last night?

"They think it's arson," said the other.

"What's arson?" asked one of the younger kids.

"That means the fire was set on purpose," I answered.

"Who would do that?" someone else asked.

Who, indeed?

The shop with the old-fashioned bicycle rusting high atop a neon sign over the building, sold more than bicycles. And Mister Robinson indulged neighborhood kids who walked in with no money to buy but letting us come in any way to look at, breath on, but not touch the dolls, soldiers, action figures and tea sets. We'd dream about the toys we wanted for next Christmas, or that we'd buy "when I get rich," we promised each other.

Who would want to burn down all of that?

Somebody will probably figure that out later, but for now, it was Christmas in June, and we eagerly pounced on the box and began pawing through the burnt offerings – tea sets with some scorched plates, dolls with singed hair and smoky clothes, slightly warped Frisbees, plastic soldiers with droopy guns, trucks and cars with a melted wheel or two. And even though I thought that I was too old for toys, I snagged a doll with a slight burn on its pink-painted cheek for myself and a charred box of plastic soldiers for my brothers.

And then it happened, again.

A vision, accompanied by goosebumps and that queasy feeling.

This time, a bolt of red, white and blue fabric unfurled in my head. A flag, maybe? After all, the Fourth of July was just a few weeks away. Whatever it was, I hoped this star-spangled vision had nothing to do with the jumpsuit lady!

With last-minute instructions given through the screen door to Ronda, Miss Milly's very pretty teenaged daughter, we headed off to King Street.

If I could look like Ronda: petite, pretty, dimpled and definitely in bloom – now that would be cool! I was yanked out of my Ronda-envy by Mama, hurrying me along past the big cardboard box, emptied of the burnt toys that the kids were playing with in the yard, past Miss Smith's still closed store and made a left turn onto Charlotte Street. We continued past an ad for Dixie sugar painted on the side of Miss Smith's store, fading and cracking in the summer sun.

As was the neighborhood tradition – at least amongst the kids – I was supposed to peel a piece of paint from the ad as I passed it, lest I be haunted in my sleep by the souls laid to rest in the walled graveyard directly across the street behind the Second Presbyterian Church. I was getting too old to believe in this kind of thing, but just in case, I quickly snapped off a piece of the hot, smooth paint as I half ran behind Mama past the Federal Building towards Meeting Street.

We crossed the busy street, walked alongside *The Green*, where we passed people waiting to fill containers with *teejun* water that flowed naturally from a well in the middle of the square.

We stopped by the Charleston County Library long enough for me to dump my books in the book drop. I really wanted to go inside the cool air-conditioned building to get more books, but Mama was in a hurry. "You got all summer to sit in the library," she said. Maybe Mama didn't have visions like me, but could she read minds?

We turned right and headed north onto King Street, and there it was…the blackened store front of the Robinson Bicycle Shop. A police officer instructed us to cross the street, and we did, joining a small cluster of people on the sidewalk who were standing and staring.

Wisps of smoke were still coming out of the store, trailing up to the rusted bicycle, unperturbed atop its neon sign.

A fire truck was parked half on and half off of the sidewalk in front of the store. The street was running with water. A heaping pile of wet cardboard boxes was clumped in the road on the Hutson Street side of the store, where I could see some people from the neighborhood standing on the side of the library.

There, I saw Tommy and his brother Sammy. Mister Mooney, who was leaning on a cane and standing next to Mister Longs, who had a jug of teejun water in each hand. I saw the Shelton brothers: Charlie, Kenny and Terry, and their sister Annie; I also saw Miss Milly's son Darren, and her other daughter, Pat. Pat saw us and waved; I waved back.

"We better get going," Mama said.

Edward's Department Store was teeming with people. Even though the name said "department store," Edward's wasn't really a department store – at least not like the nice ones – Condon's or Belk's or Kerrison's further downtown on the "white" side of King Street.

Edward's was more like Woolworth's or Kress or Grant's. Bright fluorescent lights shining on shelves and bins and display boxes crammed with cheap stuff.

"I don't know what I was thinking coming to Edward's on a Saturday morning," Mama frowned as we stood in the door, staring down aisles overflowing with people. The patrons were mostly black people and a few of what I had heard some of the grown-ups call *po' crackers*, who were glumly pawing through the shelves and bins and display racks like everyone else, while acting like they hardly ever shop at Edward's and couldn't stand to be shopping next to so many black people, when really, they were looking for a bargain just like everybody else.

Mama and I wove through the bargain bonanza of flip flops, frying pans, house coats, hampers, dishes and dust mops, navigating around people digging through bins piled high with shoes hitched together with rubber string, trying to find their size. Colorful beach balls were threatening to bounce out of their metal corrals. Were we going to the beach this summer? One of those balls would be nice.

Before I could ask, we reached the clothes aisle, with racks crammed with brightly colored summer tops, shorts and sundresses.

And there they were, the girls of my cool girl dreams – Lisa, Sherry and Rosemarie – nonchalantly flipping through a rack of summer tops.

I froze. But Mama, oblivious, headed on down the aisle alone, plopping stuff into a hand-held plastic shopping basket as she went.

Lisa, Sherry and Rosemarie giggled and chattered as they held halter tops up to chests that were way more developed than mine, turning this way and that, getting each other's opinion on how they looked.

Mama was almost at the end of the aisle. I was hoping that maybe she would go to the next aisle and I could quietly and quickly ease over there to join her before the Project Girls noticed I was there.

"Dottie!"

Unfortunately, I had no such luck.

"Girl, stop that lollygagging around. You need to pick out a gift for Antoinette's party so we can get outta here. You see those lines? Come on!"

"Yes, ma'am," I mumbled, embarrassed. I slid shyly past the Project Girls and the rack of summer blouses.

"Hi, Dottie," one of them said, as they all giggled.

"Hi," I mumbled, walking past them with my head down, which caused me to bump into Mama. The Project Girls giggled even harder.

"These girls with you?" A white saleslady, with pursed red lips and matching red hair, appeared on the aisle, scowling at Mama.

"Uh, no," Mama said, frowning back at the saleslady and glancing over at the Project Girls and the rack of blouses. "Just this one." She tugged me with her into the next aisle.

"OK girls, I'm going to have to ask you to leave the store. Now!" I heard the saleslady bark at the Project Girls.

"Hmmm! We don't want nothin' from this cheap store no how," said Lisa.

"Those are some no-manners having, fast little girls," Mama whispered. "If I ever catch you acting like that in public, I will wring your neck." No need, I thought, because I was about to die of embarrassment right now!

"Got a gift yet?" Mama asked, snapping me out of my death spiral.

Truth is, I didn't know what to get Antoinette that she didn't already have.

Mama, anxious to speed things along, grabbed a box of hankies, three in a pack, each monogrammed with a cursive "A" in the middle. "This is the kind of stuff her mama would like," Mama said, tossing the box in the basket.

Who cares what Antoinette's mama would like? But I think Mama was being sarcastic. She thinks Antoinette's mama is a snob.

Getting up to the register to pay for the white monogrammed handkerchiefs and the other stuff Mama had in her basket took forever, and once we got to the counter, the white salesgirl was snippy as she hurriedly rang up our purchases, shoved them into several bags and slapped Mama's change down on the counter. She did not hand Mama the bags.

"Hmmm. If I wanted this kind of service, I could have gone downtown to the better stores," Mama grumbled. She snatched the shopping bags off of the counter, handed me one of them and we squished through the crowd for the door.

"I thought I told you girls to leave this store!"

Mama, angry about the rude cashier, stalked out of the door without a backward glance.

But I turned around at the sound of the frosty voice.

Coming up fast toward me were the Project Girls. Behind them, buried back in the crowd but plowing forward, was the red-headed, red pinched-lips, and now red-faced saleslady.

Lisa bumped into me on her way out, throwing her arms around me as if to give me a hug, and pulled me one aisle over. She then reached under her blouse, tugged out one of the summer tops that she and her friends had been admiring earlier, and stuffed it into my bag!

"See you outside!" With a wink, Lisa waltzed out the door. Sherry and Rosemarie were already on the sidewalk, waiting.

I stood in the aisle, shocked. The sales lady whizzed past me and ran out onto the sidewalk to yell some not so nice things at the now fleeing girls.

Mama was already out on the sidewalk, frowning at the running girls and the flustered sales lady. She finally noticed that I was not behind or beside her and marched back into the store to unstick me from my spot.

"Girl, if you don't come on!" She grabbed me by the arm and dragged me out the door.

We headed back the way that we came. More people had gathered on the sidewalk across from the burnt-out bicycle shop, including the Project Girls. But while everyone else was staring at the building, the Project Girls were staring at me and Mama as we walked by. And, standing a little too close and staring at the Project Girls, was Dugga. Did they not notice him there, leaning toward them on his good leg, practically drooling on them?

Rumor had it that a too-close encounter with a train ruined the other leg, but having a bad leg didn't seem to slow down his reputation.

When he would shuffle by through the neighborhood, all the adults sitting on the bench were very solicitous.

"How you doing there, Mister Dugga?"

"Awrightman. Awright, everybody. Ladies?" He'd tip his dirty baseball cap and flash a jack 'o lantern smile, as he dragged on by.

Out of sight of the adults, the boys mocked his walk, the girls giggled nervously behind their hands and the adults tried not to stare. When the adults were sure that Dugga was out of earshot, the warnings would come. "You girls stay away from him and those warehouses on East Bay Street. He's fresh and there is no telling what he'll do to you if he catches you down there by yourself." But the Project Girls didn't seem to notice fresh Dugga noticing them, and Mama didn't seem to notice the Project Girls noticing me.

"Hey, Dottie," one of them said. I mumbled a "hey" back but kept on walking. The shopping bag with the contraband blouse in it might as well have been on fire itself. I felt that if everyone turned from staring at the smoking building and looked at me, they would see the blouse burning a hole in the bag.

And with all the police standing around because of the fire, I thought for sure that one of them was going to run over at any moment and haul me off to jail! But what do I do with this blouse? Pull it out and toss it at the Project Girls as we walked past? With all these people around? Wouldn't Mama notice and wonder why I was tossing clothes into the street?

Before I could decide what to do, Dugga shouted out, "Hey, there, Miss Carrie!" Dugga tipped his cap toward Mama and went back to feast his eyes on the Project Girls.

"Cool" Case Study #3

Cool	Not Cool
The Bench	Not actually being able to sit on The Bench because the older kids take all the seats when the adults aren't there.
Christmas in June	Playing with misfit toys from the burnt-out bicycle shop
Having lots of neighborhood friends	Having Dugga wanting to be one of your neighborhood friends
Shopping on King Street	Shoplifting on King Street
The Project Girls know my name	The Project Girls know my name!

4 CHOICE OF COLORS

When we got home, Nette was sitting on the bench, waiting for me. "Come on in out of that heat, Antoinette," offered my mother. I wish she hadn't. I was a little embarrassed to have Nette come inside my house, because although Nette lived right around the corner on Charlotte Street, it might as well have been a world away from the way that we lived on Elizabeth Street.

Nette followed us inside and sat gingerly on the sofa in our plastic-covered living room.

While Nette was getting stuck to the sofa, Mama and I went to her room to dump the contents of the shopping bags onto her bed.

And there it was – the blouse Lisa had shoved into my bag, a red, white and blue halter top. Suddenly, I got that queasy-stomach feeling that I get when my visions seem to align with reality. The bolt of red, white and blue fabric that was waving around in my head – could it be this blouse?

Mama snatched up the blouse and frowned. "That rude cashier, so anxious to get us out of her face, she probably shoved this in our bag by accident. At least I hope this was an accident, because…" Mama's voice trailed off as she dropped the blouse back on the bed and began pawing through her purse, looking for the receipt.

Should I say something now?

"I hope Miss Rude Thing didn't charge me for this." Mama quickly scanned the receipt and found no blouse among the items that had been rung up.

"Good. And I'm too busy to take it back. That's what they deserve anyway for having junky check-out counters and hiring cashiers who don't know what they're doing because they are so busy being rude." Mama tossed the blouse at me. "It's yours."

I stood there, holding the blouse. What am I supposed to do with it now? As if hearing my thoughts (because truthfully, sometimes I think she can), Mama opened a shopping bag and said, "Here. Put it in here with the handkerchiefs for Antoinette. Take it to your room, and then you can go over to Antoinette's."

A sigh, in unison, from both of us.

Antoinette lived in a huge, white, double-porched house on Charlotte Street. I had been inside her house a few times, but I'm the only one in the neighborhood who had. "I guess her snobby mama finds you acceptable," Mama once said to me.

Nette was considered the richest black kid we knew, on account of her daddy owning a moving company and wearing a suit and tie all the time, even in the summer. Her mama was a real nurse, not a nurse's aide, over at the Charleston Medical Hospital.

We swung through the wrought iron gates, up the marble steps and onto the first of the two porches that stretched the length of the house.

Nette pushed through the big *Charleston-green* painted front door with the brass handle, a knocker, and a big oval of glass in its center and we stepped inside a house that looked like something out of a magazine.

We were immediately enveloped in a comfortable coolness and the faint scent of roses. Polished wood floors stretched down a hallway and into rooms to the left and right, interrupted by antique-y looking furniture that was nothing like the dark green living room set and mismatched stuff that we had over at my house. In front of me were stairs that marched up and up, then curved out of sight.

Antoinette sailed down the hallway, making a left through a dining room with a chandelier dangling over a table that looked bigger than Daddy's car. I stood marooned at the front door. I've been to

Nette's house a few times, but I couldn't remember: Am I supposed to take off my tennis shoes at the front door? But I didn't have on any socks! And what if my feet were dirty and sweaty? Would I leave sweat marks all over this shiny wood floor?

Realizing that I was not following behind her, Nette did an about face and returned, grabbed me by the arm and unmoored me from the front door.

"Come on!"

I was tugged through the dining room, where I was careful not to bump into anything, and into a kitchen that had so many cabinets, I would have had to label the doors to figure out where stuff was.

At the sink was a woman, with her back to us. She turned. I've seen Antoinette's mom, and this was not Antoinette's mom.

"Hey, Elmira." Nette hugged the woman by the waist. Her hands were doing something in the sink, so she didn't hug back.

"Hey, Miss Antoinette. You hungry?" she asked.

"Yeah. Elmira, this is my friend Dorothy. Dottie for short. She's going to help me plan my party."

The woman turned to look at me. She smiled. She had an Afro. Not as big as Angela Davis's (or Miss Jumpsuit from the bar), but an Afro just the same, and she was wearing an apron. "Hey, Dottie for short. You ladies want a sandwich? I was just about to make some peanut butter and jelly for my kids."

Without waiting for us to answer, the woman quickly whipped up quite a few sandwiches with assembly-line-like efficiency and brought two plates over to the kitchen table where we had taken our seats. She had cut off the crusts and cut the sandwiches into four squares. Then she brought milk in glasses so nice, I was afraid that I would drop it and break it.

She heaped the rest of the sandwiches onto a big plate and exited the kitchen into a room with a wall of windows and a door that opened into the backyard. As soon as the screen door slapped behind her, three small kids and an older one all ran out of a plain, two-story house that sat far back in the yard. The last time I visited and I noticed the house, Nette said her dad had bought it, but no one was living there. I guess that had changed. The kids listened to the woman for a moment, took the plate of sandwiches and headed back into the house.

I didn't want to ask too many questions, but I wanted to know about her and she was now headed back across the yard to the kitchen.

"Who is that woman?" I blurted out.

"Oh, our maid." Antoinette said nonchalantly, as she continued eating her sandwich.

I tried to nonchalantly continue eating my sandwich too, but my mind was twirling. They…have…a MAID??? When did they get a maid? And why did they need one? I guess cleaning this big house would require such a person. But black people with a maid?!?!?

Just wait until I tell Mama this! She would need to know nothing more about Antoinette and her family to justify her calling them snobs. Which is not fair to Nette, who was really down to earth. But sins of the parents, I guess.

Elmira the maid was back in the kitchen.

"Elmira, we are going up to my room to plan my party." I had been hiding my shock at Antoinette addressing the woman by her first name with no "Miss" in front of it. Maybe maids didn't get that courtesy? I wouldn't know.

"OK, you girls don't dirty up, up there. Your mama called and she's coming home with guests soon."

Antoinette's was the only family in the neighborhood that I knew of who had a phone.

We took a set of stairs off of the kitchen instead of the curving stairwell at the front door and ended up in a long hall with closed doors on either side. Antoinette opened a door into a pink-painted room with a princess bed, all dressed in a white ruffled comforter, with pillows in ruffled cases and a ruffled canopy floating on top. There were ruffled white curtains at the windows. Through a door I saw the pink bathroom.

The pink-and-white princess room contrasted with Antoinette's usual appearance – a round-faced, unkempt girl, with wild hair (even though it was always straightened) and a pair of glasses that sat crooked on her face because she kept dropping them, sleeping on them or sitting on them.

Antoinette took a sheet of paper from a stationery set on a small white desk near the window.

"Let's sit in the playroom."

Across the hall, was a room devoid of furniture, but filled with toys that Nette probably didn't play with anymore – dolls, balls, a huge dollhouse by the window, a tricycle, boxed games, a pink guitar and more – all strewn about, on or near a big round area rug. Now, this room looks more like Antoinette!

We cleared a space on the rug and began to party plan.

"What kind of music?" she asked. "James Brown? Aretha Franklin?"

"Sure," I mumbled.

I agreed with whatever she said, because truly, I was distracted. I always liked coming to Antoinette's house and sitting in her bedroom, looking around and imagining what it would be like to have my own room, with not one, but two closets filled with clothes and shoes. I could even have my own playroom. There was no spilling cardboard box of toys or old shoes crammed in like the one closet that I shared with my brothers.

"Refreshments?"

"Yeah, yeah."

"There will be a cake."

"Of course."

"Oh, we can play these at the party."

Antoinette hopped up from the rug and picked her way through the mess of toys to scoop up a few board games that were stacked up against a wall, where I noticed the battered, kid-sized, cream-colored upright piano.

"You play the piano?"

"Not this one anymore. The real one is downstairs in the music room. I barely come in here now. I really want mommy to turn this into a dance studio."

Music rooms! Dance studios! Uh, of course!

The piano was missing a few keys. I plunked what was left.

"Antoinette!"

A voice floated up from the floor below.

"Oh, it's my mom. Come on!" She rushed out, but I drifted from the kiddy piano over to the ruffled window to look out. A light rain had started to fall. I could see all the way down to Miss Smith's house at the corner of Charlotte and Elizabeth streets.

There was an ambulance out front! The lights weren't flashing, and I couldn't hear a siren.

"Dottie! Come on down!"

I went out into the hallway but couldn't find the stairs where we came up from the kitchen. In front of me were the curving stairs that led to the front door. That curvy banister looked so perfect for sliding down, but I didn't dare! Besides, I was getting too old for that kind of thing anyway.

I rushed down the stairs instead and almost bumped into Antoinette's mom rushing up. She was a caramel-colored woman wearing a nurses' uniform, complete with the little white hat.

"Hello, dear. Antoinette is in the living room," and up the stairs she bustled and disappeared out of sight. I turned in the opposite direction from where Nette and I had entered the dining room earlier. Beyond the open French doors was a room with more antique-y furniture on which were perched ladies dressed similarly to Antoinette's mom, in white nurses' uniforms and hats.

Antoinette was working the room, shaking hands as the ladies made a bit of a fuss over her.

"Girl, you are growing so fast!"

"I remember when you were a little thing!"

"How is the summer treating you?"

Nobody said anything to me as I hung back by the French doors. Beyond that room, I saw another set of French doors that opened into another room, where I saw the real piano – a baby grand that seemed to be the only thing in the room.

Antoinette's mom came back down the stairs. The nurse's uniform was gone, replaced by a summer shift dress, with big yellow and black flowers splashed against a white background, and a matching belt tied neatly around her small waist. The hair that must have been pinned up under that little white nurse's cap was now grazing her shoulders in soft waves. She looked a little like *Coretta Scott King.*

She was baring a tray with glasses of lemonade, the same kind of glasses Antoinette and I had milk in earlier. Behind her was Elmira the maid, with a tray on which sat two plates, one with little sandwiches – that didn't look like peanut butter – and one with cookies.

"Ladies, help yourselves. But let's get started. Lots of ground to cover. Antoinette, walk your friend out and go up and let Elmira help you get ready for your piano lesson. Miss Fordham will be here any minute."

And with that, I was walked out of the cool, rose-smelling house and back out onto the porch and into the humid, damp air.

"Hey, you can stay on the porch until the rain stops," Antoinette offered, "but I gotta get changed for piano lessons." What was wrong with what she had on? Do you have to be dressed up to play the piano? I didn't know and that's not what I wanted to ask her anyway.

"Hey, what are all those nurses doing in your house?"

"I'm not supposed to say anything, but I'll tell you only if you promise to keep it an absolute secret." Antoinette's voice dropped to a whisper.

I eagerly nodded "yes," agreeing to keep the secret, greedy for what I was about to hear.

"They are planning a hospital workers strike."

A strike? Like the ones I saw on the news and in the pictures in JET magazine, with black people marching in the streets with signs, getting hosed by firemen and bitten by dogs sicced on them by the police? Here??? In Charleston?!?!?

"Yes. But pleeease don't tell anyone. If they do it, everybody will know soon enough."

"Antoinette!" Her mom's voice from inside the house.

"Gotta go! See you later."

And off she went, back into the big white house. I didn't want to stay on the porch by myself to wait out the rain, even if it meant I could sit on the swing hanging at the far end. I headed down the wet marble steps, out the wrought iron gate and back onto the sidewalk. When I got to the corner of Charlotte and Elizabeth streets, I noticed that the ambulance that was in front of Miss Smith's house was gone.

"Cool" Case Study #4

Cool	Not Cool
Everything about Antoinette's house	Everything about my house
Having a "mom and dad"	Having a "mama and daddy"
Having breathing room(s) and your own bathroom	Having your bratty brothers breathe down your neck in your too-small bedroom and busting in on you in the bathroom
Having a cute blouse	Having a cute blouse that I didn't pay for
Annette's mom's wavy black hair that makes her look like Coretta Scott King	Coretta Scott King's sad face
Having a maid	Having to help mama do a lot of the housework because "you're a girl, and the oldest and you will need to know how to do these things some day"
Calling a grown up by their first name with NO "Miss" or "Mister" before it	The pop in the mouth I would get for calling a grown up by their first name with NO "Miss" or "Mister" before it
A strike in Charleston that could make the pages of *JET* magazine	A strike in Charleston that could make the pages of *JET* magazine with pictures of people I know getting hosed by firefighters, bitten by dogs and beaten by police

Extra Cool: That godawful Star Trek series has come to an end (June 3, 1969). Nobody's boldly going with the Starship Enterprise anywhere anymore!

5 WALK ON BY

Miss Smith was found dead in her house last week, which explained the ambulance I had seen from Antoinette's playroom window. The death was all that anyone talked about for days, taking center stage as the number one hot topic once the grown-ups settled on the bench in the evenings, swatting away mosquitoes with handkerchiefs, hands and fans, as they speculated on the details of the demise of Miss Smith.

The toy store fire was still on the list of things to chew over, but the impending hospital workers strike hadn't come up yet, not even as a rumor. I was proud of myself for being able to keep a secret and for knowing something that the grown-ups didn't know, yet.

So, without anything new to chew on, they talked about Miss Smith, starting off the conversation by respectfully remembering the dead – how Miss Smith always had a smile on her face and how she would give away treats to the kids. We kids, gathered at the periphery of the bench, all exchanged knowing glances. We knew the treats were stolen by the older kids, some of whom were gathered around the bench at that moment, giving us the eye – daring us to tell the grown-ups the truth.

The grown-ups would then move the conversation from the "respect for the dead" phase to the "morbid curiosity" phase. Who called the ambulance? How did they get in? And how did they get the body out without anyone in the neighborhood seeing? "It was a rainy evening," someone recalled. "We were all inside."

What was the condition of the body? How long had she been dead? When was the last time that anyone had seen her in that store? Did she have family? What became of her cats, and did the cats – uh, make a meal of Miss Smith before she was found?

"Everybody knows that cats do that kinda thing!" Somebody chimed in, never mind that no one among us owned a cat, and in fact most of us (not me!) were afraid of cats because of the belief that cats were bad luck, or downright evil.

Were the cats still in there? A pause in the conversation as everyone looked over their shoulder toward the Smith house.

A high rickety wooden fence upon which the grown-ups rested their backs as they sat on the bench separated our yard from Miss Smith's yard. The Smith house was dark.

"Was that a cat I heard howling?" asked one of the older kids. And just like that, Miss Smith, her death and her three (possibly flesh-eating) cats got added to the neighborhood folklore, a list of haunted and/or cautionary tales that included but was not limited to the restless souls that supposedly roamed the cemetery of the Second Presbyterian Church around the corner and, of course, the warnings about bad-legged Dugga.

I hated to admit it, but the death, coupled with the toy store fire (and yes, okay, maybe the thing with the Project Girls at Edward's, even though nobody knew about that except the Project Girls and me) did add some excitement to a summer that I thought would be about as boring as bleach. And it was still only June! And the strike, if that were to happen, hadn't even happened yet. And I still had Nette's party to look forward to this weekend.

I was looking forward to getting out of the house too. A couple of weeks had gone by since the thing with the jumpsuit lady at the Nugget and it was still *Ice Station Zebra* at the house. Dinners had turned into frosty affairs with Mama not talking to Daddy, and Daddy not talking to anybody. The boys prattled on, oblivious. I walked around with a knot in my stomach, waiting for the next explosion. Daddy stomped in and out, presumably on his way to and from work. Did he dare go back to the Nugget now? Mama bustled around, doing housework, leaving only to go to the laundromat or maybe to her best friend Miss Leah's house, or up the road to GEX with Daddy to buy groceries. She couldn't drive, and he hated grocery shopping, so they always went together.

We were sometimes taken along for the ride but were left in the car while they went inside the store. I sat in the back with the boys.

On the way there, total silence in the front seat, except for the radio – Joe Simon singing something about *"The Chokin' Kind,"* as the *poomp-y* smell of the smoke belching from the North Area factories wafted through the open windows of the car.

Mama did march us all off to church last Sunday, this time without Daddy. Normally, we would wear our swimsuits under our church clothes on summer Sundays, in the hopes that Daddy would take us to Folly Beach after if we begged hard enough. It wasn't a sure thing, but sometimes he would say yes, and we'd whip off our church clothes to reveal the swimsuits underneath, grab our towels and run to the car before he changed his mind, or Mama, who was afraid of the ocean, and always thought of a reason why we shouldn't go.

But instead of the beach after church, we walked over to Grandmama and Granddaddy's house over on West Street, where Mama spent most of her time in the back bedroom, talking to Grandmama. Granddaddy showed us how to play Blackjack and some other card games, even though it was Sunday, and later walked us across the street to buy treats from a lady who was running a makeshift store out of her kitchen.

No formal invitations were sent out for Antoinette's party. I relayed a verbal invitation to just a few of the neighborhood girls, some around our age, some older.

These girls were really *my* friends and didn't know Nette all that well, but since she didn't know very many girls outside of Sacred Heart (the Catholic school she attended), and most of them were white anyway, and if she wanted more kids at her party than just me, she had to include the other neighborhood girls. No boys allowed, though.

All of the girls gathered around me at the bench at the appointed time on the day of the party and we walked over to Antoinette's house together. I felt kind of important, leading our group of seven girls to the party at the big Brooks mansion (well, it was a mansion to most of us!)

Even though they were not invited, a clump of the neighborhood boys trailed behind us anyway, stopping and watching from the sidewalk as we walked through the wrought iron gate and up the marble stairs.

The maid, Elmira (Miss?), greeted us on the porch at the top of the stairs. So, the party was going to be on the porch and not in one of those fabulously furnished, rose-smelling rooms that I saw a few days ago? I couldn't tell if the other girls were disappointed they weren't going to go inside.

"Welcome. I'll take your gifts," the maid said. I was the only one in the group with a wrapped present. I handed over the handkerchiefs, wrapped in white tissue paper. There was no card and no ribbon. A few of the girls had birthday cards, with probably a dollar stuck inside.

"Hey, Miss Brooks," we said, almost in unison as we stood awkwardly in the middle of the porch, watching as Antoinette's mom swung through the screen door and onto the porch.

Like a white woman, no one called Antoinette's mom by her first name, even with the "Miss" in front of it. Nobody seemed to even know her first name, anyway. Even her husband called her Miss Brooks, like he was doing now: "Miss Brooks, ask the young ladies if they would like some punch." To one side of the porch, Mister Brooks, dressed in a suit and tie, stood over the glass punch bowl that I saw in the china cabinet in the dining room of Antoinette's house the other day. The bowl was filled with punch with a ring of ice with fruit frozen inside floating in the juice.

"Yes, Mister Brooks. Ladies, would you all like some punch? Please have a seat and I'll get you some. Antoinette will be down shortly. She can't decide what to wear."

What to wear? I hoped she didn't come down dressed up, because all her guests were wearing summer shorts and tops, flip-flops, sandals and dingy tennis shoes.

The party guests took seats on wooden folding chairs around two small, circular, wooden tables that were covered in white tablecloths. Miss Brooks was at the other end of the porch near the swing, helping Mister Brooks fill punch glasses. The food – finger sandwiches (tuna, pimiento cheese, lunchmeat), fruit salad, potato chips, cheese curls, nuts, party mints and a white-iced, three-tiered cake trimmed in pink frosting was on the table with the punch bowl.

The other round white table held my gift, the assorted birthday envelopes, and thankfully, a few other presents, probably from her mom and dad. There were pink and white streamers entwined around the porch railings, and pink and white balloons taped along the porch columns.

After serving us punch, Mister and Miss Brooks each took a glass for themselves and settled down on the porch swing.

Awkward! We sipped our punch silently and stared at them as they stared at us; we all occasionally stared over at the boys on the sidewalk, staring at all of us through the bars of the wrought-iron gate.

Finally, Antoinette slammed through the screen door, followed by the maid and the two little girls (of the four kids I saw in Nette's backyard the last time I was here).

Antoinette was wearing a white cotton A-line dress trimmed in pink, just like her birthday cake. Her hair was done in tiny curls and pushed back from her forehead with a pink grosgrain head band; white sandals completed the outfit. I noticed that her mother was wearing the same dress, complete with headband but with white pumps instead of sandals and her ever-present string of pearls. They looked like mother-daughter models in a fashion magazine.

"Hey, everybody! Thanks for coming. I brought down some games that we can play, or we can dance. Or we can dance later after we eat? Whatever. Let's have some music. Hi!" (This was to the boys at the gate). "Mom!?!? Music!"

On her daughter's command, Miss Brooks hopped up off of the swing and went to the record player, which was sitting on what looked like a plant stand in the corner opposite the food. She lifted the needle, and Sly and the Family Stone urged everyone to *"Dance to the Music."*

Everybody was too shy to be the first to dance, so we politely played games and sipped punch. Pat, Ronda's bratty little sister who is a year older than my brothers, was the first to venture over to the refreshments to load up on sandwiches and chips, nuts and party mints; the rest of us followed. In the middle of all this munching, playing board games, milling around and tapping our feet to the music, the gate creaked open.

All heads whipped around. Had the boys breached the perimeter?

Just one boy, Darren (Ronda and Pat's little brother), who was a year younger than my brothers. He scampered up the steps and mashed himself to the side of his oldest sister.

"Darren, go back outside of the gate. You're not invited!" Pat yelled at her brother. But Darren only clung tighter to Ronda and began to whimper.

"Oh, he can stay," said Miss Brooks.

Grumbles of protest from the other boys could be heard from those left outside of the gate. Mister and Miss Brooks shared a look and a few whispered words before Mister Brooks said, "Pipe down, fellas. Alright, you all can come in, but I expect each and every one of you to behave like gentlemen. Got it?"

The boys nodded in silent agreement and began charging up the stairs, just as Miss Brooks lifted the half-empty punch bowl and instructed Elmira the maid, to collect all the glasses. Mister Brooks and Elmira followed Miss Brooks with the sloshing punch bowl into the house. The boys, once let into the party, were suddenly attacked with a case of shyness and stood frozen at the top of the stairs, not sure of what to do next.

Lucky, one of the older boys and the leader of the pack, broke through the group and surveyed the scene. All the girls, including Nette, considered Lucky to be the best-looking boy in the neighborhood. Lanky and with a curly Afro, he exuded an effortless cool. He even smoked when the grown-ups weren't around and he was going to high school in the fall. I guess I could agree with them that he was the best-looking boy in the neighborhood.

"Nice party, Miss Antoinette," Lucky said to the birthday girl. "Thank you," Nette mumbled, catching a case of shyness herself. "Congratulations on your 13th birthday. Care to dance?" He made a sweeping gesture with his right hand toward a space on the porch and we all giggled at his theatrics as he and Antoinette headed to the "dance floor." The ice broken, everybody else followed.

While we were doing the *"Tighten Up"* to Archie Bell and the Drells, Elmira the maid came back out with a tray of paper cups filled with punch. She set the tray down on the refreshment table and left again just as "Tighten Up" gave way to James Brown letting everybody know *"I Got the Feeling."*

James Brown ceded to the Isley Brothers, reminding us *"It's Your Thing,"* giving us permission to make up dance moves. Everybody took turns doing something silly. Pat did her near-perfect signature cartwheel. Antoinette, not to be outdone at her own party and apparently forgetting that she was wearing a dress and that there was no mat on the floorboards (like in gym class), did forward tumbles down the porch, her motions causing the record to skip. The boys waited expectantly for her dress to fall around her waist, hoping to see what lies beneath. But what they saw were the pink shorts that she wore underneath her party dress.

We finally collapsed to the floorboards, with Sly and the Family Stone now on the turntable, explaining that they were just *"Everyday People."* We were all dizzy and the porch ceiling appeared to be moving. Everybody was breathing hard, laughing hard and talking all at once. Antoinette's party on the porch seemed like it could go on forever.

Until…

"Y'all call that dancing?"

More interlopers at the gate – The Project Girls! Two of them, anyway: Lisa and Sherry.

We all stood up and stared down at the girls on the sidewalk. Antoinette's head whipped from them, back to me. She did a quick up and down scan of my outfit, and then whipped her head back to the girls on the sidewalk again, no doubt noticing that Lisa, Sherry and I were wearing the same red, white and blue halter top. The only difference was that I had paired my top with cut-off blue jean shorts and dirty Keds, while they wore matching white hot pants and *Hercules sandals*. Did they help themselves to those from Edward's, too?

"Ain't you gonna invite us into your party?" Lisa asked the gape-mouthed Antoinette.

Before Nette could answer, Miss Brooks came through the screen door, followed by Mister Brooks and Elmira the maid.

"Sorry, girls," said Miss Brooks. "The party is by invite only. Move along."

But they didn't.

"Tighten Up" started to play again on the record player and the Project Girls tightened it up, right there on the sidewalk: Sherry, twisting her hips and whipping that Indian hair, which was combed out and flowing like a waterfall over her shoulders and down her back. Lisa, with her big Afro, was bouncing around so that her hair and her ninnies jiggled in time to the beat.

The boys, (and Mister Brooks!) stared, mesmerized.

Miss Brooks gave a disapproving nudge to Mister Brooks and marched over to the record player and lifted the needle. "I said move along, girls."

Lisa shrugged. "Who wants to come to your ole kiddy party, anyway? Come on, Sherry. Let's see what's happening on Tiedemann Park."

The girls moved slowly past the wrought iron fence, watching us watch them deliberately *switch* their boonkeys as they walked by. Lisa stopped just before the fence ended, and stared directly at me, giving me the once over the way Nette did a few minutes ago.

"Nice blouse, Dot."

Both girls cackled as if what Lisa said was the funniest joke ever, and then they took off running down the street toward the park, leaving everyone at the party staring at me and my nice blouse.

Little Darren stated the obvious, "Y'all dress the same!" If I were white, my face would have been red from being the center of attention at that moment. Before I could think of what to say to explain the matching blouse thing, I was saved by a blazing birthday cake.

"Time to sing Happy Birthday!" Miss Brooks shouted. Everyone gathered around the white cake with the thirteen candles that Elmira the maid had lit somewhere between the party guests staring at the girls gyrating on the sidewalk and then staring at my "nice" blouse.

The birthday song was sung and pieces of cake were hastily doled out by Mister and Miss Brooks and Elmira the maid.

"Well, I guess the party is over," said Miss Brooks. "Antoinette, thank your guests for coming. You've got to get ready for church tomorrow."

Antoinette stood at the gate and with help from Elmira the maid, handed out paper cups filled with leftover nuts, mints and chips as we headed home. At least that's where *I* was headed. Lucky had convinced everyone else that a trip to Tiedemann Park would be the perfect end to the day.

"Oh! Almost forgot! Wait!" Miss Brooks dashed back into the house and came out with a stack of papers. "Be sure to give these to your parents." We each got a flier that read:

HELP US ORGANIZE TO STRIKE

FOR OUR WORKERS IN WHITE!!!!

WE DEMAND

EQUAL PAY * EQUAL JUSTICE * EQUAL RESPECT

FOR ALL HOSPITAL WORKERS!

ALL INVITED TO ORGANIZING MEETING

JULY 13 AT 7 O'CLOCK P.M.

EBENEZER BAPTIST CHURCH

(CORNER OF CHARLOTTE & ELIZABETH STREETS)

JULY

In the Country

6 THINK

Just as Miss Smith's death bumped the toy store fire off the top of the hot gossip list – the impending strike had now taken center stage – at least at the bench.

However, in my house, the imminent, annual summertime arrival of the New York relatives was all the focus.

A contingent of aunts, uncles, cousins and assorted distant relatives who had long since left Charleston to live *up North*, would pile into one or several cars for the caravan home.

Their arrival always meant roving house parties, with trips to *Skeetah Beach* (for the grown-ups only) and the annual family cookout, usually at *Riverside Beach*, thrown in there somewhere before it was all over and they all piled back into their cars to head back to New York.

These were Daddy's people – "a noisy bunch," Mama would say out of Daddy's earshot, who got noisier as the party wore on and the bottles got emptier.

Mama and Daddy seemed to have called a truce of sorts, and all hands were on deck to clean up and spruce up because, apparently, our house was the first stop on the roving house party list. I was glad for the distraction, though. I hadn't seen Antoinette since her party and had yet to explain the matching blouse thing, nor did I want to explain it!

"I should have stayed in New York myself," Mama mumbled, snapping me out of worrying about the blouse.

We straightened up around the living room that didn't really need straightening up anyway, because nobody was ever in there. Mama, talking to no one in particular, had lapsed into the one hundredth retelling of the fabulous life she could still be living in New York City if she'd just stayed up there when she moved to live with an aunt in Manhattan after graduating high school, instead of letting Daddy convince her to come back to Charleston to get married (insert big sigh here).

Before she could get to the part about how she liked to spend days walking block after block of New York City, the relatives from off let themselves into our little apartment through the unlatched screen door.

"Hey, hey, hey! Carrie, where y'all at? Why is it so quiet in here? You done put them kids to bed already? Tell 'em to get up, 'cuz the aunties are HERE!"

I'd know that voice anywhere! Daddy's sister, Aunt Thalia (Tally for short), with her learned New York accent, which was not powerful enough to overcome her Charleston drawl, switched into the house on a wave of perfume, cigarette smoke and something in a plastic cup.

She was followed by Daddy's other sister, Aunt Diane (Di for short). No New York accent for her. When Aunt Tally bolted to New York the day after graduation, Aunt Di stayed behind in Charleston.

They were both dressed in bell-bottom pantsuits and their faces were made up for a night out. Mama was wearing a house dress and a scarf that covered the paper rollers in her hair.

"Carrie! How are you, girl? How all these babies? You ain't pregnant again, are ya?" A pat on Mama's stomach and a raspy cackle. "When the Lord said to be fruitful and multiply, He didn't mean just you and Paul, you know!"

As if on cue, Daddy popped out of the bedroom. Hugs and kisses all around, and then Aunt Tally finally noticed me. "Oh, Dottie, you turning into a little lady. No ninnies yet, I see. Got your period yet?"

I was horrified – especially since this was said in front of Daddy and my snickering brothers. "Hey, no ninnies," the boys laughed.

"Where's Jimmy and Sally?" Daddy asked about another brother and his wife, who sometimes made the summertime journey home. Thankfully, the attention had turned away from me.

"You know Sally don't like no long ride," said Aunt Di, "but our brother came, along with his daughter."

"Where *is* Jimmy?"

"At the Nugget. You know him."

At the mention of the Nugget, my stomach clenched. But Mama and Daddy had their game faces on. Daddy chuckled, "Yeah, I know him!"

"Well, I will go get changed," Mama said and pivoted to the bedroom.

"Where are our cousins?" This from my brother, Peter. I had just noticed that both boys were shamelessly standing in the hallway in their underwear.

Aunt Tally turned to acknowledge the small voice. "My, you boys are growing into little men! They are all at Aunt Di's, with Nina. You will see them all at the cookout." Nina is Aunt Di's daughter. Aunt Tally's kids – Tammy, Renee and Edwin had also made the trip. So did Denise – Aunt Sally and Uncle Jimmy's daughter. I don't know about the boys, but I immediately felt left out of whatever fun that was sure to be going on over at Aunt Di's house with all the cousins over there – except us.

"Boy, you ain't got no shame standing around in your *draws*? Y'all go to bed." Daddy shooed the boys into their room. They grumbled, but dutifully complied, marching into the room and slamming the door. Normally, slamming a door would be a spanking, or at least a stern warning. But just then, the screen door banged and the house was suddenly filled with people who'd come to see the company from off – neighbors from next door and down the street – and finally, Uncle Jimmy, with a few people he'd collected from the Nugget. (Thankfully, not the jumpsuit lady!)

Daddy and his sisters went to greet the new arrivals. People milled around the living room, while I was left standing in the hallway, not sure where I belonged. Mama emerged from her bedroom, minus the house dress, scarf and paper rollers, with her short pageboy neatly combed and wearing a plain cotton sundress.

"You want some snacks?"

I nodded yes and she went into the kitchen and returned with a paper plate of chips, dip, nuts, cheese, crackers and a few little pickles. "You can sit in my room and read or something. Just don't get any food in the bed."

I sat crossed legged on the floor with a book, but my mind drifted to Antoinette's party and that darn blouse. Why did I decide to wear it? I hadn't planned to, but while I was getting dressed for the party, Mama came in and said, "Why don't you wear that cute blouse from Edward's? No need to let it go to waste."

"I dunno," I protested. "It might not even fit."

"Only one way to find out. Where is it?" I pulled the blouse, still in the bag with the box of monogrammed handkerchiefs, from the side of the cardboard toy box in the closet where I'd stuffed it. Mama helped me into the halter top, tying it in the back around my neck and waist, and guided me to the mirror over the dresser.

"You growing up," she said, with a funny look on her face. What was that look? And I didn't feel like I was growing anything, especially not the ninnies I would need to really fill out this halter top, like Project Girl Lisa.

Loud laughter brought me back to the present. I crawled over to the door, which I'd left cracked open a little. I could hear the party chatter but couldn't see the people in the living room. Cigarette smoke wafted in and so did the sounds of Jr. Walker and the All-Stars, wondering *"What Does It Take to Win Your Love"* followed by Aretha Franklin urging, *"Share Your Love with Me."*

I could see a slice of the kitchen through the cracked door. Mama was bustling about. Daddy came in, too. They worked quickly and quietly – unloading things from paper bags, putting chips and nuts in bowls, arranging cheese and crackers on a plate, taking the aluminum foil off the platter of fried chicken, pulling the potato salad out of the fridge.

I wished they would talk to or even smile at each other, or for Daddy to playfully pop Mama on the boonkey, like he does sometimes when he thinks no one is looking. But nothing.

I closed the door, laid down on the bed and fell asleep to Marvin Gaye explaining, *"That's the Way Love Is"* as I dreamed of big, halter-top filling ninnies.

I was awakened by Mama telling me I had to go to sleep in my own bed. The house was quiet. Where was Daddy? Sleeping in the smoky living room?

"Cool" Case Study #5

Cool	Not Cool
My Aunties	My aunties asking why I don't have ninnies and my period yet in front of EVERYBODY!
My New York cousins	My mom getting all wistful about the time she lived in New York City, a loooooong time ago
Mom and dad calling a truce	Mom and Dad calling a "sort of" truce -- they still aren't talking to each other
The upcoming Family Cookout	The upcoming Family Cookout
No more visions since the "red, white and blue" thing	Still getting the feeling that something bad wrong is going to happen anyway

7 IT'S YOUR THING

The arrival of the New York relatives was usually its own source of family tension, even when Mama and Daddy were on speaking terms. Daddy would be gone a lot – probably at all the house parties and cookouts and trips to the beach, or out to the *country*, mostly leaving Mama at home with us. Mama didn't go to all the gatherings but didn't like that, between work and the parties, Daddy would be gone a lot.

So, this summer, with Mama already mad at Daddy, there was no telling where this day would lead. But I was hoping for the best because I always liked these big family gatherings.

We usually gathered at Riverside Beach, across *the Bridge* in Mount Pleasant. Riverside Beach wasn't really a beach at all. Just a spot off the Cooper River with a shelly shoreline, a boat landing, an old pavilion with some rusted and rickety amusement rides and a small seating area on the edge of the marshes under trees dripping with Spanish moss. There were only a few picnic tables, so some members of the family were chosen to go out early to snag them all, that way we would have the entire picnic area to ourselves for the whole day.

But last year, the grown-ups responsible for getting up early and going across the Bridge to lay on the tables, failed to get up in time, so Plan B was to move the whole thing out to the country on the farm of an aunt and uncle on Daddy's side of the family.

That aunt and uncle, whom everybody simply called "Auntie" and "Uncle," were a slightly hunched couple, both of whom sported missing teeth and matching tobacco pipes that they smoked nonstop.

They seemed really glad to see us. But after we turned their front yard to mud playing with the well water pump all day, and somebody let the pigs loose and they rampaged through the picnic area, and we used the bathroom in the woods because everybody was afraid to go in the outhouse because of the possibility of snakes, and the boy cousins thought it was funny to yell "snake" anyway whenever the girls and women did venture into the woods when nature called, causing cousin Nina to run out with her panties around her ankles, and after Aunt Tally, near the end of the day, and fueled by too many mayonnaise jars filled with homemade "tea," decided to shimmy up one of the live oaks in the front yard and couldn't get down without Daddy's help, we never had another family gathering there again.

This year, the relatives who were supposed to get up early to secure the tables must have done their job.

Daddy, with the help of some of the older boys, and Mister Walter from next door, hitched up his small boat to the back of the car he had backed into the yard, being careful as he pulled in past the low concrete wall that separated the yard from the sidewalk. The boat had to be tugged close enough to lock it down onto the hitch.

Then the car, with the boat on back, loaded up with kids and coolers, and what seemed like half the house, was driven out of the yard, the boat bouncing, bumping and swaying as it was pulled out onto the street. I always thought the boat was going to slide off the hitch. But again this year, the boat stayed intact as we headed down Elizabeth Street, hung a left onto Charlotte, a right onto Meeting Street and onto the ramp to the Bridge headed for Riverside Beach for this year's family gathering.

The other family members had beaten us there.

Aunt Di, the "Organizer of Everything," was in full swing, directing anyone with free hands to help haul stuff from the various cars to the picnic tables.

We arrived just in time to see "the thing with the watermelon," which, like Aunt Tally getting stuck up the tree last year, was sure to become a part of the tales told at future family functions.

Cousin Bennie made a beeline for Aunt Di's car and lifted a Styrofoam cooler with a watermelon in it out of the trunk. He should have known the situation was jinxed after Aunt Di, seeing him with the cooler, warned, "Don't you drop that cooler, because it's new AND I had that watermelon on ice since last night!"

So, what happens? Cousin Bennie, halfway from the parking lot to the picnic area, dropped the cooler! The thing cracked in half.

OK, bad enough, but at least he dropped it on the grass, and the watermelon didn't smash in half. Instead, it did a little bounce off the grass, which would have been fine, too, except the watermelon did another little bounce off the grass, and a roll, and another bounce and a roll, and another bounce. Everybody stood stock still as the watermelon continued its roll-bounce down a small slope behind the picnic area and into the marshes, where it floated for a few seconds before promptly sinking out of sight!

The first one to move was Cousin Bennie, who made a dash for the marshes to try and save the watermelon. His heroic attempts were halted by his daddy, Uncle Butchy, another one of Daddy's brothers, who, holding a stew pot in one hand, jerked his son by the t-shirt collar with the other.

"Let it go, boy."

But it was clear that Aunt Di wasn't going to let it go. She plunked down a box of plastic forks and stalked over to father and son. Ignoring her brother, she leaned right into Cousin Bennie's face.

The cousins all gathered nearby, anticipating high drama. Was she going to slap him, like she did that one time at a family gathering at her house when he got to be what Aunt Di called "too busy" and knocked over and broke one of the dozens of ceramic birds that she collected and had scattered all over the place? Cousin Bennie had taken the slap in stride, grinning and rubbing his cheek, while his daddy stood by, indifferent as he sipped on a bottle of beer. This time, instead of another slap, she hissed, "Stay away from me for the rest of the day!" And she stalked off.

"Oooooh!" This from all the cousins, including Cousin Bennie's own brothers and sisters. As Aunt Di marched by, we shrank out of her way. Uncle Butchy, indifferent still, shrugged, unleashed his son's collar from his grip, and put the stew pot in the center of one of the tables.

Who brings stew to a picnic, anyway? Aunt Harriet – who never comes to these family gatherings anyway on account of her being very religious and not onboard with the amount of drinking that goes on at these things. But her husband and children always show up, and she always sends Uncle Butchy along with a mystery pot of something that Aunt Di would pick up, like she was doing now, just as Uncle Butchy put it down, and unceremoniously plunk it on one of the far tables, where it would sit in the hot summer sun, practically forgotten, attracting only the occasional fly, which would buzz close and then, just as quickly, buzz away.

Uncle Butchy, at some point in the day, would at least gamely take one heaping plate of whatever was in the pot and eat it in a few big fork's full, making a big deal about how good it was. But the rest of us picnic guests, including Aunt Harriet's own children, would stay away from the pot, not even caring to exhibit enough good Southern manners to at least put a little bit of the stuff on our plates, only to push it around with our plastic forks and then, when no one was looking, toss it in the trash.

Aunt Harriet's mystery stew was not to be trusted, according to Aunt Di, "The Knower of All Things," because Aunt Harriet was so "out the country," you could barely understand what she says and, worse still, she was steeped in voodoo!

How else to explain how Uncle Butchy, who, even though he was short and had *conked* hair, was considered as good-looking as Daddy and all the other brothers, and could have had his pick of the ladies, ended up with a plain woman who seemed to be almost twice his height, who wore thick cat-eyed glasses and rarely left her house except to go to church? "She put a spell on him, that's what!" Aunt Di would insist. But, hey, they've managed to produce six kids between them (including Cousin Bennie), so there must be something there!

But Aunt Di's drowned watermelon, Aunt Harriet's mystery pot of stew and somebody's hard potato salad aside, there was plenty of food to choose from. Hamburgers and hot dogs, deviled eggs, cucumbers, tomatoes and onions marinating in oil and vinegar, barbecued chicken and ribs, shrimp, crabs and fish caught fresh and cooked right on the spot, potato chips, boiled peanuts and cookies. Grown-up drinks for the grown-ups and four-for-a-dollar cans of soda for everybody else in many flavors: orange sherbet, lime, grape, root beer, strawberry and cola (although the cola flavor didn't taste half as good as the real Coca-Cola, which Mama and Daddy only bought at Thanksgiving and Christmas anyway).

After all the food was spread out and the grills and steam pots and fryers were fired up, the grown-ups unfolded blankets and lounge chairs and settled in for a long day of eating and drinking and smoking and talking. Boring.

Everybody seemed to be there – relatives and wanna-be relatives, real cousins, distant cousins, and play cousins, aunts and uncles by blood and through marriage. And a few locals – no relation, but those who've shamelessly attached themselves to the caravan out to the country for a day of free food and drink.

Uncle Louis was the only one missing of Daddy's siblings, which is not unusual, as he was a bit of a wanderer, and nobody seemed to know where he was, or when he might pop up, or with whom. An old family rumor went around that Uncle Louis was once married to two women at the same time. But the grown-ups would explain it away by saying that he was *touched* and either didn't remember he'd already had a wife when he married the second one or didn't know he couldn't have two wives at the same time.

All of the cousins left the grown-ups to their boring day and escaped down to the river's edge to watch Daddy drive the car down the ramp, unhitch the boat and crank it off the trailer into the Cooper

River. As we ran through the grass and across the small parking lot to the shoreline, motherly words of caution followed our backs: "Drown, and I'll kill you!"

Some of the boy cousins made it down to the shoreline before the girls, so they got the first ride in the boat. As we waited our turn, across the water, I could see the Charleston skyline, punctured here and there by church steeples.

Denise, Tammy and Renee, the New York girl cousins, were all sporting intricately braided cornrows. Cool!

They also were wearing tennis shoes that they refused to take off, even wading in the water with them on. Despite that bit of weirdness, I thought they were the height of cool. They all sported wrists full of bracelets that jangled and clanged as they cautiously splashed about in the water.

"I like y'all hair," I ventured, shyly. "Who did it for y'all?"

"We do each other's hair," answered Renee. "I'll do yours before we leave, Dottie." Nina, Aunt Di's daughter, already had her hair braided. I was a bit jealous.

But I did like the way the New York cousins said my name, which came out as "Dahdee" in their New York accents. Very cool!

"Come and get it! Food's ready!" The lunch bell, in the form of my brother Paul, had been sounded. He came running down to the shoreline just as Daddy motored back with the first boatload of boys.

The first round of eating was for the kids and any adult who couldn't wait. Then we'd be shooed off and the adults would take over.

The boys piled out of the boat, splashed through the shallow water onto the shore and ran up to the picnic area. The New York girl cousins and Cousin Bennie's two sisters, Eva and Opal, not wanting to be associated with eating with "the kids," decided to take their turn in the boat.

With a lot of giggling, squealing and jangling of bracelets, the gaggle of girls waded through the water and were pulled up one-by-one into the boat by Daddy. Cousin Nina, who was getting on my nerves trying to imitate the New York cousins' accent, wanted to go too, but she was on age with me (actually, a year older), so she should be eating with the kids, whether she liked it or not. Besides, Daddy said the boat was full, so we had to wait until later. Anyway, I was hungry!

By the time we got back to the picnic area, the eating was in full swing. I'd been waiting for a grilled hamburger since the end of last summer! I slathered the bun with mayonnaise and mustard, loaded on the pickles and dumped some chips on the side. I'd save the 'cukes and tomatoes for later, when I eat some of the boiled shrimp, and maybe a crab or two.

"Hey, hey, hey!"

In the middle of all this eating and talking and flirting and dancing and telling old jokes and listening to Peggy Scott and JoJo Benson on the radio tempting each other with a *Lovers' Holiday*, up the grass strolled Uncle Louis.

Cheers went out as he made his way across to the picnic area.

"Man, where you been?"

"What happened to you the other night at Paul and Carrie's?"

"We were beginning to think you had gone the other way to New York!"

Uncle Louis was immediately surrounded by people, as if he were a movie star; and he could be, too. Of all the brothers, he may be the most handsome, although I'm sure they would have argued the point. He had really white teeth and a sly smile that made him look as if he were always keeping a very naughty secret. Uncle Louis had a beard, a mustache and sideburns that were so intricately conjoined and neatly shaven to his face, it required a bit of staring at just to get the lay of the thing.

"Wait!" Uncle Louis said as Aunt Di tugged him toward the food and the coolers of drinks.

"I brought someone along I want y'all to meet. Hope it's OK. Where she at?"

He reached behind him and pulled forward a woman in red hot pants, white stack-heeled espadrilles and a blue halter top cut so deep in front that her halter-top-filling ninnies threatened to plop out at any moment. A clanging armful of bracelets, fake eyelashes that extended all the way to the shoreline, too much makeup for a day at a cookout and a weirdly colored Afro wig – reddish-brown and black – completed the look.

"Hey, everybody, this is Vera. Say hi to Vera."

Vera got an enthusiastic "Hi!" from the men and boy cousins. The ladies stared and frowned.

Oh. My. God. It's the lady from the bar!

My stomach coiled into a nervous knot and I couldn't finish the hamburger I'd been waiting all year to eat. Of all my visions, I didn't see this one coming.

Miss Vera (now I know her name; not cool!) minced her way through the picnic area, tottering along on her stack-heeled espadrilles, waving an armful of bracelets as she swatted away bugs.

"No doubt the cheap perfume," Aunt Di sniffed as if she just smelled some bad fish.

"I like her heart bracelet," Cousin Nina whispered to me. She just would! I caught a glimpse of the bangle – a filigree of golden hearts circling her wrist, meeting at a solid heart-shaped clasp. I hated to admit that it was pretty.

Uncle Butchy made a beeline over to Miss Vera and introduced himself. He was so short that he only came up to the "V" in Miss Vera's halter top, a height he no doubt would consider perfect.

Miss Vera perched herself on the edge of a picnic bench and smiled her overly lip-sticked smile at no one in particular. I was hoping she got a splinter in her boonkey wearing those short shorts!

The men were buzzing around Miss Vera like the flies around Aunt Harriet's stew pot, but Miss Vera was not looking at them as she scoped the picnic area. Was she looking for Daddy?

She seemed oblivious to the scowls directed at her from all the women, except Mama, who sat, seemingly frozen, in a lawn chair. Like Miss Vera, she, too, was staring at nothing in particular.

Uncle Louis, too, seemed oblivious to the havoc he'd brought to the picnic. "Hey, Vera. What you want to eat? Plenty of food here, girl. I know you want to keep fitting into those hot, hot pants, but have a little somethin'!"

At the offer of food, Aunt Di sprang into action. "Oh, where's my manners?" She smirked as she walked over to the Mystery Pot, opened it and heaped a big clump of…whatever!... onto a paper plate. "Here, have some of this," she said sweetly, offering the plate to Miss Vera. "Made it myself," she said, cutting off Uncle Butchy, who was about to rightfully give the cooking credit to his absent wife.

All eyes were on Miss Vera, who had enough manners to at least take a small bit of the stuff before washing it down with a big gulp of whatever Uncle Butchy had hurried over to the cooler to get for her. She left a lipstick mark on the can. "I'm really not hungry at all," she said and plopped the plate on the table. The men surrounding her laughed and grinned like Miss Vera just made a big, funny joke.

Oh, Lord! I couldn't stand to see Mama sitting there with that frozen look on her face. So, I bolted.

I ran down to the parking lot and stood around, huffing and puffing, trying not to cry or throw up, or both.

How could Uncle Louis do this?

OK. Maybe he didn't know. After all, he lived – who knows where he lived! He surely couldn't be faulted for not knowing the ins-and-outs of all our family drama.

Maybe he stopped by the Nugget, and there was Miss Vera, who probably pushed herself up on him with her big… wig. And maybe she was mad – ticked that Daddy wasn't coming to the bar as much anymore after I saw them. And getting a whiff of a rumor that the family cookout was about to happen, maybe she wrangled an invite as his date. Yeah, maybe.

I had all this stuff swirling around in my head and nowhere to put it. I ran toward the waterfront to get away from my thoughts, but Daddy was down there, pulling up in the boat and helping the girls out and onto the shore.

I didn't want them to see me, so I turned and ran toward the old pavilion, and the rickety rides baking in the Fourth of July sun. No one was there right now.

The old white man who ran the rides would often appear as if by magic around sunset at the now locked metal gate, tobacco-stained and half-drunk, ready to take our quarters and acting as if he were doing us a favor by letting us get on his groaning merry-go-round, lopsided Ferris wheel and creaky swing ride.

I scooted between a gap in the gate. I couldn't see Daddy at the boat landing, nor could I see the picnic area, but I could hear music and laughter, muffled now as I walked further into the little amusement park.

There seemed to be less of the park than I remembered from the year before. Beyond the rides were empty spaces beginning to overgrow with grass. Off to one side were a few empty and falling apart game booths. A faded face caught my eye – an old woman's face painted on the back wall of one of the booths. I walked over for a closer look.

She was wearing a headscarf decorated with little suns, moons and stars. She was festooned with many painted-on necklaces, including one with a hand dangling from it. She stared down at me with one eye, the other one lost to chipped paint.

"Hey, ole fortune teller, what can you tell me?" I asked out loud.

The faded red lips didn't part, but I heard: "I tell you what, little darkie girl. The park is closed right now. But you can come on back here and wait with me 'til it opens."

I shrieked and backed away from the booth and that nasty, raspy voice. "Come on, girlie," the voice beckoned. I ran back towards the entrance and hauled myself up and over the gate this time, instead of crawling through the bars. Big mistake. I snagged my left arm on a piece of rusted metal sticking up at the top of the gate. I screamed and fell to the dusty ground on the other side, but scrambled up quickly and kept running, now crying and bleeding, blood dripping down my arm.

I saw Mama and Daddy in the parking lot up ahead. As I got closer, I could hear that they were arguing.

Mama: "What are you trying to do? Embarrass me in front of your family? Well, it worked!"

Daddy: "What are you talking about? I ain't bring nobody!"

Mama: "No, you get poor Louis to do your dirty work!"

I wanted to scream out to them to shut up and help me, but I was out of breath. They didn't see me until I ran straight into them and collapsed at their feet. Mama screamed.

The scream brought everyone down from the picnic area. And there I was – bloody and dusty – and bawling about a fortune teller and a voice and an old fence, and… and… and…

"Poor chile is hysterical," someone said.

"Maybe she needs some water," said someone else.

"I think maybe she gonna need some stitches," said Aunt Di, M.D. The adults mumbled and nodded in agreement.

Somehow it was decided that the quickest way to get me downtown to the Emergency Room was by boat, straight across the Cooper River to the Charleston Harbor.

Daddy picked me up, bloody arm and all, and walked down to the boat landing. Mama followed, shouting instructions to the crowd following behind us for someone to watch the boys and for the boys to stay out of trouble until we got back.

Once in the boat, Daddy wrapped my arm in a clean piece of cloth. As we shot across the river, the crowd at the boat landing and the rickety amusement park got smaller and smaller, and the Charleston skyline got closer.

Daddy pulled up close to a small dock at the end of Calhoun Street and steadied the boat while Mama climbed out. Daddy then hauled me up to her on the landing.

"Hey, sweetie, you gonna have to make the short walk to the hospital. Daddy'll come pick y'all up after I go back and hitch up the boat and get the kids. You'll be fine. You daddy's brave little girl, right?"

WHAT?!?!?

He wasn't coming with us? And why was he talking to me like I was five years old?

"What??? You're not coming with us?" Mama exclaimed.

"What am I supposed to do with the boat?" Daddy said. "The Emergency Room ain't that far and she ain't bleeding that bad. I think she just scared, is all. Look, I'll pick y'all up after I gather up the kids." And with that, Daddy made a swift turn back to Riverside Beach.

The city was quiet, with virtually no traffic as we walked down Calhoun Street toward Charleston Medical Hospital.

"I look a mess," Mama complained. "I hope nobody I know sees me. And I sure don't feel like a long wait at the hospital."

But as expected, we waited in the emergency room for a long time before seeing a doctor. I didn't cry when I got the shot to numb the area around my wound and I didn't turn away as the doctor put in the stitches.

"My, you're a brave little girl," he marveled. That's because I am NOT a little girl, I wanted to say. But I kept quiet. I wanted to tell Mama something, anything to break the silence.

"Antoinette's mom is a nurse at this hospital," I told her after the doctor finished the stitches and left the room.

"Nurse's aide," Mama mumbled.

"Huh?"

"She's a nurse's aide. Not a nurse."

"But Antoinette said the black nurses are gonna…"

Before I could finish, the doctor came back in.

Daddy never came back to pick us up. I heard him explaining to Mama late last night that after he got back to Riverside Beach, the other kids who didn't get a ride in the boat wanted a ride. And somewhere in there, he had to eat. And then it got later and the amusement park opened, and the kids didn't want to leave until they got on all the rides, and before you know it, the day was done.

While all this was happening, Mama and I took a cab home from the Emergency Room. We spent the rest of the day moping around and waiting for the sound of the car backing into the yard with the boat attached.

We heard them, alright. A loud scrap and a thud brought us running to the screen door. The boat and trailer were sitting on the sidewalk, detached from the car. Daddy sent one of the boys to get Mister Walter next door to help him hitch the boat back up to the car.

"Must have bounced off when I hit the curb," Daddy explained as the two men lifted the boat back up onto the trailer.

"Looks like your chain broke," said Mister Walter.

"Serves him right," Mama muttered before going into her bedroom and slamming the door.

"Cool" Case Study #6

Cool	Not Cool
All the food at the family cookout	Mystery stew
My New York cousins and their New York accents	Having Charleston cousins pretending they have a New York accent
Cornrows	Having one of my Charleston cousins getting her hair cornrowed before me
Family	People pretending to be family
Bracelets	Miss Vera's bracelets
Watching the sun set from the top of the Ferris wheel	Missing the sunset ride on the Ferris wheel (and, yeah, the creepy guy who runs the Ferris wheel)
Riverside Beach	Having my day at Riverside Beach cut short (No pun intended!)

8 TIME IS TIGHT

I got six stitches, which made me the center of attention at the bench the next day. The older kids allowed me to take a seat as everyone gathered around so I could show off my stitches.

My brothers, jealous of my place at center stage (center bench?), tried to take the spotlight off me by prattling on and on about the cookout and the boat ride and the amusement park. Big deal! Who needs to ride some old rickety rides anyway? I was getting too old for that kind of thing. And I could do without seeing that creepy old park operator or hearing his creepy voice ever again. I could do without seeing Miss Vera ever again, too.

I never told anyone why I was running out of the park in the first place that day. And nobody at the house talked about Uncle Louis bringing Miss Vera to the family gathering.

My stitches and the cookout were now a week old, and the rally about the strike was still a few days away.

Today, the spotlight had shifted to my New York cousin, Renee, and her flying fingers, as she plaited row after row of tight braids onto my head, her bracelets jangling to the rhythm while she worked. I was no longer at center bench but sitting on one of the wobbly chairs to the side, so Renee could move around my head as she braided, while I winced in silent pain.

It was now or never for getting my hair braided. Our house was the last stop for the roving band of relatives before the New York crew piled back into their cars and hit the road tonight for the long drive back to New York City.

Inside, the adults were laughing and drinking and talking and dancing and eating. Occasionally, someone would poke their head through the screen door with several dollars dangling between the fingers of an outstretched hand to ask one of the kids – anybody's kid – to run down to Costa's for plastic fruit-shaped containers of lemon or lime juice or a bottle of ginger ale or a big bag of pretzels or a few dill pickles or packs of chewing gum. The rush to that outstretched hand would be fierce because the kid who reached it first knew that, for his or her services, the generous adult would say, "Keep the change!"

I was restricted from this money grab and had been so for over an hour now, anchored to this chair and hovered over by a crowd of kids who were moving in closer and closer to get a good look at my hair being transformed by Renee's precision parting, and a dab of Royal Crown hair grease, from a puffy, knotted mass to shiny, neat rows of braids that lay flat to my scalp.

"Oh, that sure takes a long time to do. Does it last long?" someone asked.

"Oh, it can last about a month," said Renee in her thick New York accent.

"That looks really tight. Does it hurt?" asked someone else.

"A little bit," I mumbled.

"How you gone get them knotted-up things out of your head?" Still another question.

"It'll be easy to loosen out," Renee assured. I didn't care. Ever since I saw Cousin Nina with braids at the family picnic, I was determined to have them, too. No pain, no gain!

And my getting my hair cornrowed was a consolation prize of sorts, which didn't really make up for the big prize – getting to go to New York City, like Cousin Nina.

I was really mad about that. They invited me to come, too, but Mama didn't think I had enough new clothes to be going out of town, especially to New York. So off Nina will go, with her hair freshly braided, lugging several pieces of her mama's good red American

Tourister suitcases, crammed with new stuff bought just for the trip. Spoiled brat!

The next adult to poke a head out the screen door was Aunt Tally.

"Y'all come and eat!"

The "y'all" was for my brothers and me, the New York cousins and the Charleston cousins.

As the kids rushed inside, leaving the envious and hungry neighborhood kids at the bench, Renee finished off a braid. "I'll finish the rest after we eat," she promised.

We were herded into the kitchen, but not allowed to touch any of the food, which was spread out buffet-style across every available surface – the stove, of course, and the counter where the dish rack normally was (the dish rack was in the sink), the counter where the TV normally was (the TV was nowhere to be seen) and the kitchen table, around which were seated adults who couldn't fit into the living room.

Mama had been frying chicken all morning. And the roving relatives brought even more chicken, along with barbecued spareribs, potato salad, tossed salad, bottles of Thousand Island dressing, dinner rolls, pots of red rice, chicken *perlo* and a huge pan of banana pudding.

Food was heaped on our plates by the adults as we shuffled past the pans and pots and dishes and pointed: "I want this. I don't want that."

We were then instructed to find seats anywhere on the floor in the tiny hallway. All the boys took over the bedroom that I shared with my brothers, where the TV from the kitchen was plugged up.

The older girls – the New York cousins, and Ronda from next door – took over Mama and Daddy's bedroom. The thinking was that because they were teenagers, they could balance plates of food on their laps without making a mess. Nina tried to go in there, too, but she was shooed out, and so had to sit in the hall with me and Pat, Ronda's little sister. Cousin Bennie came out of the roomful of boys and joined us because he liked talking with the girls anyway.

Sitting in the hall, between the living room and the kitchen, wasn't a bad spot, except for grown-ups stepping around us to get to the bathroom. But we did get to hear all the stuff the grown-ups were talking about.

The living room and the kitchen were smoky and noisy and crammed with family, friends of the family and a few of the neighbors. Then there were people, like Mister Oliver, who didn't fit into any of the above categories. Mister Oliver, at the moment, had the attention of the living room with his retelling of a tale of some long-ago fire aboard a Navy ship he'd sailed on – or said he sailed on.

Mister Oliver was mixed with something, because he looked more white than black, and spoke with a slight British accent. He was not a relative and not really a friend of the family, at least not on Daddy's side. I never knew how he fit in on Mama's side of the family, but I once overheard Daddy joking with Mama about Mister Oliver being a former flame of Grandmama's whose fire for her had not yet extinguished, and that he was still waiting around for her to change her mind and leave Granddaddy to marry him. "He could have been your daddy!" Daddy would joke. Mama would shush Daddy and chuckle at the thought.

But whoever he was to her, Mama tolerated his unannounced visits, rolling her eyes at the ceiling and sighing when she heard his voice at our screen door, expecting to be let in, expecting a seat on the green loveseat, expecting a taste from one of Daddy's bottles and expecting an ear willing to listen to his many-times-told tales of Navy adventures long since passed. Mama usually indulged him, even though, after he was gone, she complained that he talked too much, stayed too long and took up way too much of her time.

Today, Mister Oliver had the good luck to show up with a party in progress and many captive ears, beside Mama's, forced to listen to his storytelling.

Mister Oliver was so into his story, complete with sound effects, that he didn't seem to notice that the men in the audience, although goading him on, were actually making fun of him.

"Is that how it happened, Oliver?" one asked between snickers.

"So, you saved the whole ship, huh?" laughed another.

I'd heard the story so many times, I could have run into that living room and finished it myself. But Mister Oliver, undeterred and lost in a memory hazed with smoke from a massive shipboard fire, continued his tall Navy tale.

The mention of "fire" prompted a no doubt welcome change of subject.

"Say, did they ever figure out what caused that fire over at Robinson's Bicycle Shop?" A man's voice interrupted Mister Oliver.

"What fire?" Mr. Oliver asked. I saw Mama rise from her seat near the hallway and hand Mister Oliver his drink, now watered down from the melted ice. She pointed to her vacant seat, which he took, and she waded through the overflow of kids docked in the hallway and headed into the kitchen.

"Man, the fire in the store over on King Street," someone else explained. "Didn't burn it to the ground, but it was a lotta damage."

"Probably an insurance fire. You know how they are." A new voice.

"Insurance fire or not, what was the official cause?" A woman's voice.

"Who knows?" The new voice again.

I leaned forward from my spot on the floor in the hallway to see who the new voice was. Standing at the screen door, his Afro silhouetted against the setting sun, was Mister Cornell Franklin.

"You know these fire people can be like the police, too. They don't tell us nothin' and this happened right in our neighborhood."

Clucks and grumbles of agreement all around.

Mister Cornell Franklin came further into the living room. His eyes were following the backside of Aunt Tally, who had risen from her seat to move the needle on a scratched part of a record spinning on the turntable.

Mister Cornell Franklin bore a striking resemblance to *Malcolm X*, complete with horn-rimmed glasses.

"Hey there, Cornell!" The men greeted the newest guest.

"And who is this?" Aunt Tally asked, padding on bare feet back to the loveseat where she had been sitting, making a big show of elegantly tucking her legs under herself as she retook her seat.

"Oh, you ain't been gone that long! You remember Cornell, Miss Julia's son?" Someone did the introduction, or reintroduction.

"Oh, I remember going to Miss Julia's to get my hair pressed when I still lived in Charleston, but this cannot be little Cornell who used to run around the shop! May I fix you a plate?"

"Why certainly, yes. Thank you." Mister Cornell Franklin spoke like a professor.

Aunt Tally took her time uncurling her legs from under herself, standing and then slowly stretching, with Mister Cornell Franklin's gaze fully upon her, before walking like she was in no hurry to get to the kitchen to fix Mister Cornell Franklin a plate.

While she was gone, Mister Cornell Franklin started up again about the fire.

"I tell you what, this could be a long, hot summer, what with that fire and now this hospital workers' strike that is supposed to be happening. Maybe Charleston is finally waking up and joining the *Movement*."

"Y'all can keep all this agitating down South," this from Aunt Tally as she returned with Mister Cornell Franklin's plate of food. "I'm glad I'm heading back to New York tonight, away from these crazy crackers!"

"Nowhere to run, nowhere to hide, my sister," Mister Cornell Franklin responded. "You got plenty of crazy crackers in New York City. They just got more city to keep y'all on one side and them on the other. *The Man* let y'all come to the other side just long enough to work for them, or to entertain them, and then y'all back on the other side."

"Well, we all work for The Man," Aunt Tally said in a tone that sounded less inviting than when she offered to get Mister Cornell

Franklin a plate of food just a few minutes earlier. She stiff-armed the paper plate toward him and plunked herself down on the loveseat beside him with less of a show than when she stood up moments ago.

"Thank you." Mister Cornell Franklin acknowledged the plate of food being offered to him but did not immediately start eating. "Yes. Yes, most of us do work for The Man. But my mother has owned her hairdresser salon since most of y'all can remember. That's what we need – more economic empowerment, so we can tell The Man to go to…"

"Hey, Malcolm X!" Someone cut off Mister Cornell Franklin in mid-rant. "We ain't here to start the revolution just yet, my brotha. It's a party, remember? Let's dance!"

The volume went up on James Brown singing *"Mother Popcorn"* and the small living room floor was crowded with gyrating adults, much to our amusement and that of the boys who'd joined us in the hallway, and the older girls who'd finally come out of the other bedroom.

We started mocking the way the adults were dancing, particularly the weirdest one – that being Uncle Marvin, whose style of dance we aptly named "the Uncle Marvin." He was full into the thing now, bending over at the waist, rolling his balled fists around each other in front of himself while kicking his legs back one at a time. We were all doing "the Uncle Marvin" in the hallway until Mama caught us and shooed us back out into the yard.

As promised, Renee finished braiding my hair as the shadows created by the setting sun grew longer and the party inside got louder.

A game of hide-and-seek was organized and off we scattered, while the counter made a poor attempt at trying not to peek at where we were going.

The game seemed to end almost as quickly as it began and we were back to sitting on the bench in the now near dark, swatting mosquitoes and bragging about who was the better hider. The New York relatives were starting to emerge from the house, hugging the Charleston relatives, and the neighbors and friends who'd stopped by to see them off.

Luggage and food left over from the party and a Styrofoam cooler packed with seafood on hot ice to keep them fresh during the long ride back up North, were crammed into the trunks.

Renee and Tammy and Denise and Nina were packed into the back seat of one of the cars in the caravan before anybody noticed that Edwin was missing.

Aunt Tally, who was all smiles and hugs and kisses a moment ago, was beginning to get mad; a pecan-colored lady, I could see her face redden under her makeup.

The older kids suggested a search party and off we went. The hunt took us across the wall behind our house and through the lot with two abandoned and falling down houses. Out of the lot and across Charlotte Street we headed, for only a cursory peek through the wrought iron fence at the cemetery in the back of the Presbyterian Church where the tombstones cast foreboding shadows, down the red-brick walkway and through Wragg Square, then down the steps onto the sidewalk on Meeting Street, back across Charlotte Street, and past the front of the Federal Building. We took a left onto Henrietta Street, with a quick turn through the back parking lots of Citadel Square Baptist Church and Emanuel AME Church; then next, a pop out of the Emanuel Church parking lot and onto Calhoun Street, past the Greyhound Bus Station and the laundromat. We gave a glance across the street at Buist School with its fenced-in yard and then hung a left back onto Elizabeth Street, past Costa's now closed corner store, past the Nugget and back to the bench.

No luck. No Edwin.

"He might be in that graveyard," offered one of the boys. That was the one place the search party didn't actually go because, well, even Edwin wouldn't be so crazy as to hide out in there, would he? Not that we were scared to go in there, mind you, but the cemetery is a place filled with dead people buried in the dirt, and to make sure they stayed down there, they are buried in coffins, with slabs of marble thrown on top of that for good measure. And everybody knows that if you make the mistake of actually walking on, or even jumping over, one of those graves, well… any old spooky thing could happen. To ward off any bad luck, you had to get one of the kids to step on your finger on the sidewalk outside of the cemetery. And that hurt. I was getting too old to believe in this sort of thing, but you never know, so it was best not to even go in the cemetery at all.

So, Daddy went in there and, sure enough, while we looked in through the wrought iron fence, he found Edwin hunkered behind a tombstone so big, it looked like a little house, and which was, according to the words chiseled on it, "Dedicated to the Memory of Edwin Bryan, son of W.H. and S.B. Gilliland, Born in Charleston, S.C. January 30, 1844. Died in Washington, D.C. June 27th, 1864. A Soldier of the Confederacy. He Yielded His Young Life, A Willing Sacrifice for His Country."

I wondered if Edwin chose that particular tombstone because his name was the same as the dead Confederate soldier. I didn't have a chance to ask him because Daddy dragged Edwin, who was good and dirty by now, from his hiding place, and we all trooped back to the waiting cars. Aunt Tally bopped him in the head with her purse as he squeezed his dirty self into the back seat amongst the girls, who themselves were squeezed in between the stuff that wouldn't fit into the trunk.

Aunt Tally jumped in the front seat beside Uncle Jimmy and off they peeled to New York City in a plume of exhaust fumes, Aunt Tally's perfume, fresh seafood on dry ice, fried chicken wrapped in wax paper, and Aunt Tally still cursing at Edwin in her studied New York accent, seasoned with a lot of Lowcountry.

"Cool" Case Study #7

Cool	**Not Cool**
Cornrows	Really tight cornrows!
New York City	My cousin Nina getting to go to New York City and not me
Stitches	What I had to go through to get stitches!
Mr. Cornell Franklin looking like Malcom X	Mr. Cornell Franklin thinking he IS Malcolm X
Dancing the Uncle Marvin	Uncle Marvin dancing the Uncle Marvin

9 OH, WHAT A NIGHT

The slightly deflated ball lay forgotten beside the bench. We had been waiting for the day to cool to organize a game of kickball. But Daddy parked in the yard about an hour ago, taking away our "field." Besides, nobody was much interested in playing, anyway. Even the bench was forgotten, empty and leaning lopsided in the late afternoon sun.

Sitting on the bench was not the best place to be at the moment, anyway, if we wanted a better view of all the activity happening across the way around Ebenezer Baptist Church.

As far as we could see from where we stood clumped together on the sidewalk, Elizabeth and Charlotte streets were all parked up. A few TV trucks were parked around, including the Channel 5 truck from the TV station around the corner at Charlotte and East Bay streets.

I noticed a white man with a camera around his neck, jotting down something in a small notebook as he talked to people entering the church.

Police cars were parked everywhere. Were there dogs in the back seats? Were the fire trucks coming later with the hoses?

"Where is everybody?" I asked no one in particular, meaning where were the grown-ups, a few of whom would normally be on the bench by now. "At the rally," someone said.

Mama wasn't at the rally. She had gone to Miss Julia's to get her hair done. Daddy wasn't there, either. He was inside, sleeping.

No more words needed to be spoken. With no one around to tell us not to, like moths to a flame, the glop of kids, which included my two brothers, drifted down the sidewalk to the corner, closer to the church.

We stopped in front of Miss Smith's house, all but forgetting that the place was supposed to be haunted after Miss Smith died in there last month. I turned to look toward the upstairs windows. Was I expecting to see a ghostly Miss Smith peering out, curious, too, about all the commotion across the street? Only one of her cats stared back at me.

I turned back to the church. People were streaming in. I could hear an amplified voice, muffled, and then clapping – more of the voice and louder clapping, accompanied by shouts. Then there was singing, or was it praying? I couldn't tell from where we were standing. As if reading my mind, someone in our crowd suggested, "Let's get closer. We can't see nuthin' from way over here."

I looked back toward our yard. Daddy didn't say we couldn't leave the yard. But we are already out of bounds, standing down the block, and so far, nothing bad has happened. What's another corner?

We crossed the street and stood in front of the church for a few seconds. Then we allowed ourselves to be swept up in the tide of people surging inside.

Did we need to be dressed up, I wondered? Will an adult stop us at the door and tell us we didn't belong here? Was Mama in here after all? If she was, it was hard to tell. The church was packed. People were even standing in the aisles to the sides of the pews. I looked up and saw people crammed into the balcony. We got no further than the back of the church by the doors. And that may be just as well. Just about everyone was fanning themselves, either with a program, a church fan, a handkerchief or their hands. It was hot in here, indeed.

Lots of people were seated on the stage. But down in front, in the pews, was the sight to see; a sea of nurses in white uniforms, with white caps atop dark hair framing brown faces.

A man stepped to the microphone. Who was he? His rhythmic voice riled the crowd. I half-listened while I looked around the church. A few recognizable faces, but no Mama. After the rhythmic man spoke, another person stepped to the microphone and then another. I didn't recognize any of the speakers.

Then a nurse detached herself from the sea of white in the front pews and walked up the steps. She reached the podium and turned to the audience.

Miss Brooks!

I whipped my head around the church looking for Antoinette and her dad, or maybe even (Miss) Elmira, but it was hard to make them out in this mash of people.

Miss Brooks clutched several sheets of paper, which she spread out on the podium. She cleared her voice.

A baby started to cry: a mom could be heard trying to settle the kid down. Miss Brooks cleared her throat again. She looked down at the papers and back up at the audience. I noticed a handkerchief in her hand that she used to dab at her throat. It looked like one from the set I gave Antoinette for her birthday!

"Good evening," she began. "I am Mrs. Lavinia Brooks."

Lavinia! So that's her first name!

Her voice sounded a bit shaky, as if she were nervous. Miss Brooks always seemed so sure of herself when I visited Antoinette at her house.

Miss Lavinia Brooks continued, "After graduating from Burke High School, I went to New York, where I eventually became a Licensed Practical Nurse, or LPN. I returned to Charleston but could not get hired at the Charleston Medical Hospital as such because the hospital would not recognize the program in New York under which I was licensed. Because of this, the hospital didn't accept my LPN status and would only hire me as a nurse's assistant.

"I find the working conditions at Charleston Medical to be barely tolerable. We take orders from white nursing students who threaten to have us fired if we don't do as we are told. And, of course, there is the unequal pay.

"The breaking point for me and several of the nurses you see seated here this evening, came when we reported for the night shift recently and the white registered nurses on duty refused to give us a report on the patients we were to care for that evening. We, in turn, refused to go to work without knowing whom we'd be working with. Well, we were told we weren't getting a report, so we refused to take care of patients for whom we did not have the proper medical information.

"We nurses' aides started organizing. Then the other black hospital workers – cafeteria workers, janitors and such – heard about our meetings, so now we are not only nurses but also other black hospital workers. We tried to get a meeting with the president of the hospital. He agreed to a meeting date, but when twelve of us showed up at the amphitheater on the appointed date and time, everyone was there except him. Well, we thought, since he wouldn't come to us, we'll go to him. So, we marched over to his office. By this time, other black hospital workers had joined us. But he hid in a back room and never came out to speak with us. Instead, he called the Charleston Chief of Police, who threatened to arrest us if we didn't leave and return to work.

"So, we left. And here we are tonight.

"All we are asking for is fair working conditions, fair wages and recognition of people like me who have had legitimate training elsewhere to perform the duties of an LPN. And we are prepared to stay off the job until our conditions are met. Thank you."

Miss Lavinia Brooks' speech was punctuated throughout by an amen or two, and a few hallelujahs from the audience, followed by a rousing round of applause, and a standing ovation from her fellow nurses in the front pews. After the applause died down, she added, "On behalf of Charleston's hospital workers, I would like to thank the *Southern Christian Leadership Conference*, the local Ministers Alliance and the community for their support."

More applause as Miss Lavinia Brooks walked off the stage and took her seat. I guess Mama was wrong about Miss Brooks being only a nurse's aide.

Someone else stepped up to the podium and said a few more words, then the event appeared to be over because the nurses rose and silently walked down the main aisle and out the doors two-by-two. We parted on either side of the door as they walked out, followed by the hospital workers, then the people on the stage and then the rest of the church, from front to back.

Antoinette waved at me as she silently walked by, holding her father's hand. And surprise, surprise! Project Girl Rosemarie was making her way down the aisle, sullenly following her mother, known around the neighborhood simply as Sister. I didn't think the Project Girls were the church-going types, but if your mother was the self-appointed neighborhood evangelist, I guess you don't have a choice. Did her mother know of the kind of girls her daughter hangs out with? Maybe Sister was too busy roaming the neighborhood handing out religious tracts to notice or care. Rosemarie practically snarled at me as she walked by. Before I could decide if I was going to snarl back, a hand grabbed me and pulled me into the aisle.

Mama.

"Mama!?!?"

"What you staring at? You never seen an Afro before? Y'all been out here long enough. Let's go. Time for baths and bed for everybody. Daddy just let y'all run wild when I'm not around."

I kept my eyes on the back of Mama's new 'do as my brothers and I fell in line behind her and joined the mash of people emptying out of the church and onto the surrounding sidewalks.

Night had fallen, but it might as well have been the middle of the day for all the lights, cameras and action going on around us – TV trucks with lights atop, photographers with bulbs flashing, police cars with blue lights spinning, people packed on the sidewalks. And on the street, the nurses, fronted by some of the people from the stage, were forming long rows from curb to curb along Elizabeth Street, facing south toward Calhoun Street. The other hospital workers lined up behind the nurses. And supporters and the merely curious, lined up behind them.

Someone started singing, and the rest of the group joined in:

Ain't gonna let nobody turn me 'round,

Turn me 'round, turn me 'round.

Ain't gonna let nobody, turn me 'round.

I'm gonna keep on a-walkin;' keep on a-talkin,'

Marching on to freedom land.

I was now afraid. Is this where the dogs and the hoses and the bully clubs come in? These people weren't nameless faces in a JET magazine photo or blurs rushing down the street in TV news clips. These were my neighbors and family and friends. I couldn't imagine the dignified Miss Brooks getting blasted with a hose or Mister Mooney having to use his cane to fend off a gnarling dog or pretty Miss Frannie getting clubbed on her beautiful head.

The group in the street slowly started to move. But Mama, my brothers and I stayed on the sidewalk. I looked into the faces of the adults as they marched on by. They didn't seem concerned about dogs and hoses and clubs. They just sang as they walked by, resolutely staring ahead.

Keep your eyes on the prize…oh, lawd.

Oh, lawd. Gotta keep your eyes on the prize, oh lawd.

The marchers headed down Elizabeth Street.

"Come on." Mama tugged and gently pushed us into the street, and we joined the march. We passed our little apartment, where I saw Daddy and Mister Mooney standing on the little concrete porch out front. Even the Nugget had emptied out, men and women standing at the door with the neon bottle repeatedly emptying and filling with electric bubbles.

The marchers made a right onto Calhoun, toward the hospital zone. But Mama silently pulled us out at Costa's darkened corner store and we headed back to our yard, where I noticed Daddy's car was now gone.

Once inside, Mama, true to her word, hustled us through baths and to bed, only offering as an answer to my question about her hair, "I needed a new look."

"Wake up!"

Mama was shaking me awake from a dream where the Project Girls were circling me in the schoolyard, admiring my perfectly shaped Afro. I did not want to be awakened from this dream.

But Mama shook me again.

"Wake up," she says. "There's a fire!"

The boys were already running behind Daddy to the front door by the time I put on a pair of shorts under my night slip and rushed behind everybody else.

Already outside on the little concrete landing in front of the apartment were the neighbors from the other three apartments – Miss Milly and Mister Walter, along with Pat and her sister, Ronda, and brother, Darrell, from next door; Lucky and Miss Kat and Mister Mooney from upstairs, along with Miss Dot and Mister Longs, who lived next door to them.

Other neighbors had come from down the street – Miss Frannie and her daughter, Donnalee. Miss Leah and Annie, and the rest of the Sheltons. Sammy and Tommy, and their mom, Miss Betty.

We all stared at the high blaze that was finishing off the two abandoned houses in the overgrown lot across the fence from our yard.

The fire lit up the night and bathed our faces in an eerie orange glow. No one spoke, captivated by the flames licking at the sky, the smoke pouring out of the broken windows, the crackling sound and the smell of wood burning.

Where were the fire trucks? Did anyone go to the corner to pull the lever on the firebox?

Maybe someone did because I heard fire engines off in the distance. The trucks, with red lights flashing and sirens howling, pulled up on Charlotte Street. Several firemen jumped off the truck and rushed toward the burning houses.

"Do you know if anyone was inside?" The fire chief shouted at us over the low concrete wall. No one spoke. Finally, Daddy did. "No, chief. I don't think so. Both houses were abandoned. No one is usually in there except vagrants."

Daddy didn't sound like himself. His words were coming out clipped and official sounding. I don't think I've ever heard him say, "vagrants." We just called the people who flopped in those raggedy houses bums or winos.

"Chief, may I have a word?" An unfamiliar voice behind us. A white man's voice.

Everyone turned. A white man, indeed. Wearing pajamas and slippers like you'd see on a TV dad, relaxing in their recliners in front of the fireplace, smoking their pipes and reading their newspapers.

I was suddenly aware, and keenly self-conscious of how we all must look – the black residents of the four apartments and the other neighbors – in our various hand-me-down slips and old, yellowed t-shirts and frayed housecoats and draggers and head rags and scarves and stocking caps and paper hair rollers.

Daddy was actually only wearing boxer shorts and no t-shirt. Thank goodness it was dark so no one could see his hairy chest!

"And you are?" asked the fire chief.

"Thomas. Thomas Smith. I own the house next door. I'll meet you around on Charlotte Street."

No one spoke as Thomas, Thomas Smith offered up a "good night" to the group and turned toward the house of the late Miss Smith.

"Cool" Case Study #8

Cool	Not Cool
The hospital workers' strike, kicking off right in my neighborhood!	The Civil Rights Movement finally coming to Charleston, SC
No dogs, hoses or bully clubs after a peaceful rally	All the police cars surrounding the neighborhood, anyway
Miss Lavinia Brooks is a real Nurse!	Miss Lavinia Brooks, our neighborhood Angela Davis?
Mama's Afro!	Daddy not saying anything about Mama's Afro
Those run-down old houses in the lot next door finally gone!	Another fire in the neighborhood
New neighbors?	New WHITE neighbors?!?!?

Extra Cool: Man lands and walks around on the moon. (July 20, 1969).

Not So Cool: There's nothing else on TV!

10 WHAT DOES IT TAKE

Mister Cornell Franklin had co-opted one of the makeshift stools from around the bench and turned it into a makeshift stage, upon which he was standing as he bellowed into a megaphone. His backdrop was the charred remains of the two abandoned houses that burned down last night.

Standing sentry in front of him and facing the audience were men his age from the neighborhood. Silent and still, they stood, their eyes hidden behind sunglasses, their hands folded in front of them.

His audience was people in the neighborhood, young and old alike, including Mama and the twins, me and Antoinette, the Project Girls – Lisa, Sherry and Rosemarie, and that fresh Dugga, who I thought was, again, standing too close to Lisa.

I was trying to pretend that I didn't see Lisa, Sherry and Rosemarie, but Nette kept trying to catch their attention by waving at them.

"Stop!" I hissed at her, yanking down her waving hand.

"Why? I thought you guys were friends now," Antoinette whined. One contraband blouse does not friends make!

The truth is, while I idolized them and wanted to be like them, I didn't want to be *with* them because, frankly, I was really afraid of them. Lisa could beat up any girl – and probably most of the boys – at school, and Sherry and Rosemarie were her willing accomplices.

We turned our attention to the bellowing Mister Cornell Franklin.

"Look at this. Look at this!" he barked into the megaphone, not turning, but jabbing a finger at the blackened mass behind him. "That's the second fire in this neighborhood, counting the Robinson Bicycle Shop fire. I ain't never remember two fires in this neighborhood so close together.

"Now, one time, I would say it was just something that happened. But two times, and I could think somebody's doin' this."

"But who and why?" a male voice asked from the audience.

"Thank God, no one has been hurt or killed yet. But I'll tell you why, my brothers and sisters. They could be trying to burn y'all outta here."

Mumbles and nods, shuffling of feet and knowing looks were shared in the audience.

"Who's trying to burn us outta here?" The same male voice.

"My brother," Mister Cornell Franklin turned to the voice. "Look around the edges of your neighborhoods very closely. The little old white ladies like Miss Smith, with dead husbands and children grown and gone, are either too old, too broke, too stubborn or all of the above to make the white flight to the new suburbs west of the Ashley River or even to the wilds of Mount Pleasant, east of the Cooper River.

"Note that the old white ladies who refused to leave by moving van are now leaving by hearse. And come to take over their palatial digs are their children – tired of the hustle and bustle of the big cities or the uncertainty of the hippie life, and ready to play lord and lady of the manor back home in the South. Except, the view from the porch is of black people – you people – too many of you, and too close for comfort for some of them. They don't like to be outnumbered; you know. So, y'all got to go, by any means necessary. It's called *gentrification,* and it means that it's time for them to reclaim the neighborhoods that were settled by their great, great, great grand pappies, perhaps the owner of your great, great, great grand mammies. And don't look for them to thank you on your way out of here for helping them to pay their mortgages on these houses y'all been renting all this time."

This bit of speechifying drew a few "Speak, brother!" and some knowing "hmmm-hmmm's" from the audience.

But someone dared to disagree.

"With the exception of Miss Smith, all our neighborhood old white ladies are still in they big ole houses as far as I know, and I don't imagine they hobblin' around in they nightgowns and they canes settin' fire to stuff. The Robinson Bicycle Shop fire was probably an insurance fire, and those old houses went up in flames probably because of some winos sleepin' in there with lit cigs."

Before Mister Cornell Franklin could respond, someone piped in, "Wait a minute. Who was that white man in the pajamas last night anyway?"

Another neighbor offered, "He said he was from next door." All heads swiveled to a side view of the otherwise thought to be vacant Smith house. No car out front. No signs of life inside, except a cat licking its paws in an upstairs window.

An in-the-know female voice chimed in, "I heard that's her grandson, and he inherited the house."

"I rest my case," said Mister Cornell Franklin.

How did she know that? And what case was Mister Cornell Franklin resting anyway?

"Come on! You don't think this guy is running around the neighborhood at night setting fires, do you?" A male voice.

"Not in those pajamas!" someone else said. Everyone laughed.

"But why did he have to talk with the fire chief in private?" Another neighbor remembered.

Mister Cornell Franklin, seeming to not like that the conversation and the attention were moving away from him, yelled, "What they had to talk about that couldn't be talked about in front of us, huh? I tell you what, they all work together. Maybe this fire chief helping them set these fires. And after that big hospital workers rally, you know, they probably thinking we getting beside ourselves."

Silence from the audience now.

"Maybe… maybe the fires are to scare us. Put us back in our place. Well, they didn't turn the hoses and the dogs on us after that rally. Can't have a polite little southern city like Charleston appearing on national news being mean to their Negroes. But what better way to intimidate you than to scare you into thinking that these neighborhoods, filled with all these old wooden houses, could be set ablaze on any given night?"

Heads swiveled left and right to regard the old wooden houses along Charlotte and Elizabeth streets and over on Henrietta Street.

Then voices tumbled over each other as neighbors anxiously expressed out loud the possibility of these streets becoming late-night infernos. Mister Cornell Franklin lowered his megaphone and nodded silently as he observed the paranoia he had just unleashed.

After a few minutes, he raised his megaphone again.

"What are we gonna do? Are we gonna let ourselves get burned out of our own neighborhoods? I say it's time to fight back – enough of this marching stuff. We're just going in circles. Time to stop and take a stand. Time to start the revolution!"

Mister Cornell Franklin's call to arms drew more anxious chatter and a smattering of applause, which seemed to displease Mister Cornell Franklin, who shook his head in disgust.

He raised his megaphone to speak again, just as a police squad car zoomed up, its siren letting loose a few warning whoops.

A white police officer stepped out of the car but did not approach the crowd, which was quickly dispersing, some headed for the safety of the bench on Elizabeth Street. Thankfully, the Project Girls headed off, too, without incident.

"Awright, let's break this up, y'all hear? Franklin, you have been warned about assembling without a permit. You not gone get another warning before I haul you in, ya hear?"

Mister Cornell Franklin stared at the cop for a beat longer than was probably wise before slowly stepping off his "stage," and handing the crate to Mama, who was standing near the front.

"Sister Carrie, I see your 'fro is as beautiful as the day my mother styled it for you. I am so glad you have freed yourself from the bondage of the hot comb and have embraced your African birthright and your natural crowning glory."

Mama self-consciously patted her hair with one hand while taking the crate with the other.

"Thank you, Cornell," she said to Mister Cornell Franklin, as he retreated down Charlotte Street, not giving the cop another glance.

I stood staring incredulously at Mama, who, if she were white, would be red-faced with blushing right now.

"Hey, you gotta come to my house today!" Antoinette's voice snapped me out of wondering what the heck was happening to Mama.

"Huh?"

I turned to her.

"Come to my house. No one's there. Mom's off doing that strike stuff and Elmira had to take one of her kids to a doctor's appointment."

"I, uh...."

I was trying to think of a way to get out of this. I wanted to go because maybe Antoinette will tell me some stuff about her mom being a nurse in New York, but I didn't want to be grilled about the Project Girls.

"I should ask my mama," I finally said, purposely letting Mama walk away from us, the crate in her hands and a twin on each side of her.

“OK. I’ll go with you.”

Oh, Lord! I was hoping she’d just go on home and wait to see if I showed up.

We turned the corner onto Elizabeth Street and the bench was overrun by grown-ups – from the apartments and around the neighborhood, taking up every available seat, with kids buzzing around.

All the talk was about the strike, and the fire last night, and the other fire at the toy store and whether any of these events were in any way connected. Kids were leaning in close to hear the discussion and they weren’t being shooed away.

“First, Mister Robinson’s store. Now, those old houses.”

“And this second one right after the strike.”

“A coincidence? I don’t know.”

“But why Mister Robinson, though. He one of their own.”

“Yeah, but he was one of the first to welcome us in his store. None of that go through the back door stuff.”

“I know what. We got to stand firm and support these hospital workers. Dr. Martin Luther King Jr. died for us. We got to carry this thing on. ‘Bout time sleepy ole Charleston woke up and got involved.”

"How is your mama, chile?" An adult turned from the conversation and turned to Antoinette. We were standing around with the other kids and I was waiting to get a word in to ask Mama if I could go over to Nette's house.

"Fine," Antoinette answered.

"She sho' did a nice job last night up there at the church," said another.

"Thank you," Antoinette mumbled shyly.

I was embarrassed for Antoinette to be the center of attention because I knew I would have been with a bench full of grown-ups questioning me and staring at me.

Me, to the rescue: "Mama, can I go over to Nette's for a little while?"

"Uh, sure, baby. Just don't get in Miss Brooks' way over there."

Antoinette let herself into the unlocked front door and we headed to the kitchen to make peanut butter and jelly sandwiches.

I barely got the jelly on the bread when she started in on the Project Girls again.

"They sure have more breasts than we do."

Who says breasts? Everybody calls them ninnies, but Antoinette *is* a nurse's daughter.

"Do you think they are in their right grade? Maybe they've been left back a few times; that would explain the breasts. I wonder if they have boyfriends. Mom wouldn't even think of letting me wear hot pants like that!"

I chewed while Antoinette talked and talked and talked.

Should I tell her about how I ended up with the same red, white and blue halter top as Sherry and Lisa? Maybe not. Even though I know stealing is wrong and I should have told Mama where the blouse really came from, I was afraid she would have been mad at me for not telling her sooner, like in front of the store, and she wouldn't have let me go to Antoinette's party. When she said I could wear the blouse, I should have said no, but… it was a cute blouse and I'm tired of wearing the kiddie stuff Mama picks out for me when we go shopping.

"How did you end up wearing the same blouse as them?"

The question I'd been dreading.

"Oh, there was a whole rack of 'em at Edward's. A dime a dozen, really. Practically a steal."

"Cool!"

What could I say? Maybe the less Nette knew, the better. I had to admit, though, that it was kinda cool that Antoinette thought I was cool enough to know how to dress like the Project Girls, until...

"Hey! Maybe we should go over there?"

"Over where?" I asked around a mouthful of peanut butter and jelly bread.

"Over in the Projects. I've never been over there. Maybe we can find – what are their names? Maybe we can find those girls and kinda hang out with them. They did like your blouse, and they did try to come to my party."

Here we go again! Am I about to let myself get dragged again to some place where I shouldn't be and didn't want to be?

"Nette, I dunno. I am not supposed to go over there."

"Who would know? We'd just walk over and just walk around a little bit and see if they are outside somewhere. If we don't see them, we can come right back. Okay? They'll be glad to see you. You're practically their friend!"

Well, noooo…but…

So, we left the calm and clean and quiet and cool of Antoinette's rose-smelling house, headed to the Concord Street Projects.

Why didn't I just say no? I guess I still wanted her to think I was kinda cool, even though it was hot as heck out here. But there we were on the Projects, tromping around on walkways that cut through overgrown grass that surrounded row upon row of identical bungalow-style houses the color of dried mustard with clotheslines festooned in the back.

"Antoinette, let's go. Nobody's out here," I said, just as we turned a corner and came upon…

Miss Vera.

The big-Afroed, pant-suited, painted lady from the bar. The bangled and braceleted lady in the stack-heeled sandals from the picnic. Except, she didn't look so glammed up or coolly dressed right now. No makeup. No Afro. Just a dingy-looking housecoat, with a scarf tied around her head, bare feet, a basket of laundry under her arms and two small, dirty-looking kids running around her ashy legs.

The kids stopped running around to stare at us. "Hi," one of them offered. Miss Vera gave me and Antionette a brief, disdainful up and down glance, before ordering the dirty kids inside and following them into one of the mustard-colored bungalows.

Without a word to Antoinette, I about-faced and stumbled out of the Projects, headed home.

"Do you know her?" Antoinette asked, as I hurried, hot-faced, toward Charlotte Street.

I didn't answer.

As we made our way out of the Projects, out of the corner of my eye, I saw Mister Cornell Franklin deep into an animated conversation with Dugga, waving around the bullhorn he still had in his hand as he spoke. What could those two have to talk about?

AUGUST

Cool/Not Cool

11 GOING IN CIRCLES

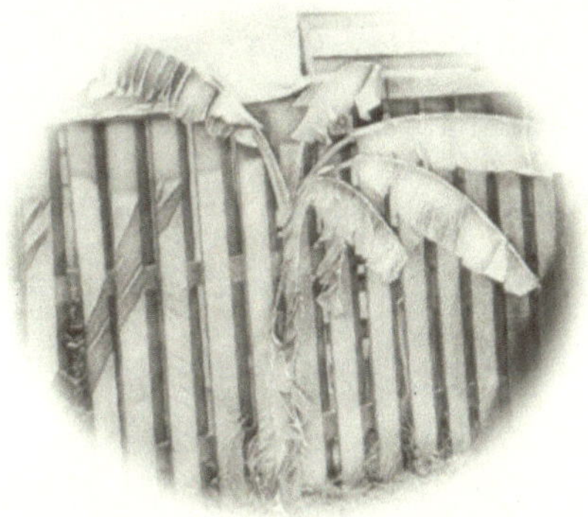

The hospital workers strike dragged on into August, and now the garbage men decided to throw their own strike! As garbage piled up around the city, including the mess squirming with maggots in our own backyard, my own Mama has decided to join the Movement!

Not that she told us anything directly; I found out like I seemed to find out most things around here, listening in – this time, from the hallway last night while Mama was in the kitchen talking to her friend, Miss Leah, who had stopped by after we (well, my brothers!) had gone to bed.

"I've made up my mind. We are going," I heard Mama say.

Going where?

"I will miss my friend," said Miss Leah. "I wish you well. But how you gonna swing it with four kids? That's a lot to ask of your aunt, to look after all them kids while you go to work."

Work? Mama's getting a job?

And didn't Miss Leah mean three kids? There were only three of us. And which aunt? Granddaddy has some sisters who lived out in the country on John's Island. Grandmama's people lived even further out, south of Charleston off U.S. 17 in a little town called Yemassee.

Wait! There was that aunt who…

I absentmindedly slapped at a mosquito biting into my thigh. "I know if somebody don't go to bed and stop trying to get into grown folk business, that skeetah ain't the only thing that is gonna get slapped tonight!"

I eased back into the bedroom, but didn't close the bedroom door, because it was too darn hot anyway, even with two fans whirring in the room. I could still hear them talking, lower now, so I had a hard time hearing.

My mind was racing. The only aunt Mama would even think about living with was Granddaddy's sister, who had escaped to New York a while ago. This was the aunt that Mama went to live with during her self-described magical year in New York City after high school, and before Daddy convinced her to come back home to Charleston to get married.

Hmmmm…wait! Are we moving to New York City?!?!? Without Daddy?!?!?!?

"Sorry, I can't watch your chirren this time, Carrie." Miss Leah was now in the little hallway, leaving. "I would send one of my kids, either Terry or Annie, over, but we all going over to the revival at my church tomorrow. I do wanna hear what Pastor has to say about this strike stuff. What about Ronda?"

"No, Milly said her chirren going to Vacation Bible School at their church." A sigh from Mama. "That's all right. I will figure out something. Maybe take them over to Mama's. I'd hate to spend the money on a cab, though. But that's the quickest way to get them all over there and still make the rally at County Hall. I promised Cornell I'd help him. . . ."

Did she mean Mister Cornell Franklin?!?!? They are on a first-name basis now?

"Well, you be careful out there. Those people…"

As they walked to the front door, their voices faded away and so did I.

I dreamed that I was in an episode of *A Family Affair*, living in the same New York City high-rise as the twins Buffy and Jody, their sister, Sissy, their Uncle Bill, and the butler, Mister French. I was at their door, come over to play with Buffy and Jody. Mister French answered the door and led me through the beautifully decorated, spacious apartment toward the children's bedroom. We turned down one hallway after another, Mister French and I, endlessly on our way to my play date with Buffy and Jody, with that theme music playing along the way – *da, da, da, dut-ta-dut-ta-dut-dut...*

Mama woke me up the next morning before I ever got to Buffy and Jody's bedroom door.

And now she was hustling us up to drop us off at Grandmama's, so she could march the streets with Cornell.

"Go get my address book," Mama yelled from the bathroom,

where she was picking out her Afro. And what in the world is she wearing? Hot pants!?!?

"Hurry up!" Mama snapped me out of my staring.

The address book was really a stenographer's pad, with addresses and phone numbers written in no particular order on the pages and scraps of paper stuffed in the back – ads torn from phone books, articles torn from newspapers and magazines and recipes she wanted to try.

The pad was usually on the nightstand on her side of the bed. It was 11 a.m., according to a turquoise-colored clock radio that sat on her nightstand. Almost the middle of the day, in the middle of the week. Where was Daddy? At work? At the Nugget? At Miss Vera's dried-mustard-colored bungalow over on Concord Street?

"I don't know what's taking so long to get my notebook," Mama yelled, this time from the kitchen.

"Coming!" I yelled back.

What is becoming of this family? Daddy and Miss Vera. Mama and Mister Cornell Franklin. Are we indeed moving to New York? And where is that dang pad? I rummaged through the pile of magazines, newspapers, bills and books on the nightstand, finally finding the pad. Frustrated and angry now, I snatched it off of the table, causing the odd bits of scrap paper to fly out of the pad and onto the bedroom floor. On top of the pile was an ad torn out of a phone book for a lawyer, one who specializes in, among other things, divorces.

I kneeled down to stare at, but didn't touch the ad.

"Girl, if you don't pick that stuff up and get moving, I will put some fire under your boonkey," Mama said, now at the bedroom door. "Let's go."

We hurried past the bench crowded with kids and down Elizabeth Street past Costa's store. We took a right on Calhoun to the Greyhound Bus station, where Mama called a cab from the pay phone in the waiting room.

We jumped into a Safety Company cab when it arrived a short time later, Mama up front and me and the boys in the back.

"West Street, please," Mama said to the cab driver.

And then, nobody spoke. James Brown was on the radio urging us to *"Say it Loud, I'm Black and I'm Proud!"*

As we headed toward Grandmama and Granddaddy's house, I could hear Mama flipping through the pages of the pad that she pulled from her handbag. Was she looking for the ad for the divorce lawyer?

My head was spinning and my stomach was churning. Are Mama and Daddy getting a divorce? Are we really moving to New York City to live with Mama's aunt? Does this aunt live near my cousins Renee, Denise, Tammy and Edwin? Will I see Buffy and Jody walking along Madison Avenue with their older sister Sissy, with Buffy clutching her Miss Beasley doll?

How would we even get to New York, anyway? Mama didn't have a car, and I doubted that Daddy would give her his. Besides, she didn't even drive. Would we squeeze into the caravan of cars headed back North after the next visit from the New York relatives? Or maybe we'd take one of those Greyhound buses humming in front of the station?

It would be kinda cool, though – me becoming a New York City girl. Wouldn't my cousin Nina, Antoinette and the Project Girls be jealous of that?!

I'd wear my hair in all the fabulous cornrow styles that my cousins would create just for me. I'd jangle a wrist full of bangles and bracelets, bought from a vendor right off of the streets, like my cousins. I'd eat Nathan's hot dogs while I'm walking down Broadway with my cousins, talking to them in my "new" New York accent. They'd take me to Coney Island and I'd be the cousin coming down to visit little old dusty Charleston for the summer. Wouldn't that be cool?!

Except, I wouldn't be around Charleston to make Nina, Antoinette and the Project Girls jealous of me. They'd only see me in the summers – the only time I saw my New York cousins. They wouldn't see my cornrowed hair or my bangles or hear my "new" New York accent, except during the summers. So, what would be so cool about going off to New York if everybody in Charleston was going to forget about me as soon as I was gone?

The cab pulled up to the only house left on West Street, a blue wooden one-story thing, with dark blue shutters, which was set well back from the street and fronted by an overgrown yard with a giant banana plant right in the middle of it all.

Through all this greenery waded Grandmama, pushing back a banana leaf with one hand, and with her ever-present pipe in the other hand as she walked towards us unloading from the cab.

"Well, look here. All my grand babies come to see me!"

We trooped through the jungle that was Grandmama's yard, up the porch and through the screen door to her living room, where we were greeted with the smell of pipe tobacco and still more plants, in flowerpots, jars and plastic containers, sitting on top of everything.

"Mama, when are you going to get tired of being the only person left on this street in this old house and move to one of those nice apartments at Robert Mills Manor they just built across the street?"

"Don't start on that again. I'm not movin' in that cinder block project housing mess and neither is your daddy," said Grandmama.

"Your friend, Shirley moved in. How is she doing, by the way? Still working at that motel?"

"Ya, she is. She sees all kinda things over there and finds all kinda stuff too. Ya daddy's still at work, by the way," said Grandmama, drifting from one topic to the next, as she hugged and kissed each one of us.

"You forgot Chick still lives across the way. He keeps us company," Grandmama said, jumping back to the topic of moving. "He say he ain't goin' nowhere, either."

"He needs to move too," said Mama. "His house is about to fall down around him too. You know those people ain't trying to fix up these places. They're just waiting for y'all to finish paying off their mortgages and then they'll kick y'all out, so they can sell these properties to the highest bidder, like they did the rest of these old houses on this street. Charleston's changing, I tell you. And if they have their way, they'll move all of us black folk back out to the country and back on the farms."

"You sound like that agitator you been runnin' around with," said Grandmama, puffing on her pipe and regarding Mama, her Afro, hot pants and hoop earrings.

I actually thought Mama looked cool, even though I didn't like the cab driver flirting with her while we were getting out of the cab.

Mama, ignoring Grandmama's comments about the agitator and her disapproving look at Mama's outfit, grabbed her by the hand.

"Mama, can we talk for a minute – in the bedroom?"

"What about? I wanna spend some time with my grandbabies!"

"About this." Mama fished around in her handbag and pulled out a scrap of paper that she showed to Grandmama.

"Oh, lawd, chile!" Grandmama read the paper and rolled her eyes at the ceiling. "Y'all go on outside," she said to us. "I gotta talk some sense into ya mama here. Stay in the yard!" And off they went to the bedroom.

My brothers dashed out of the door into the jungle. I pretended to follow behind but let the screen door slap shut with me still on the other side of it. With the fear of Mama giving me a whipping for eavesdropping again almost forgotten, I eased toward the bedroom and crouched behind a tall plant growing in a plastic bucket in the little hallway.

"Look Mama, I really need a favor," I heard Mama say. "I got this meeting I'm supposed to be at. And, well, I really don't want to take the kids. I mean, it'll be a lot of people and anything could happen…" Mama's voice trailed off.

"Oh, I know about that big rally at County Hall. You think I don't know what's been going on around town, just because I don't get out like I used to? Frankly, I don't think that's no place for a woman in your condition and with three babies already. Anything is liable to happen."

"Please keep your voice down," Mama whispered.

Undeterred, Grandmama continued, "Instead of running around half-dressed following that Pied Piper, you and Paul need to patch things up."

"Mama, I really don't have time to get into this right now, but if you know so much, you must know about …"

"Oh, I heard about the cookout at Riverside Beach, and the uninvited guest, even though you didn't invite me or ya daddy."

"Mama, you know I can't stand to be around those loud people any longer than I have to and neither can you. Look, the time is going. Are you watching the kids?"

"About this uninvited picnic guest …"

"Mama, I really don't want to talk about this anymore."

"Well, if you weren't in such a hurry, I could tell you what Shirley told me about the uninvited picnic guest, who she saw down at that motel where she works…"

"Wait." Mama cut Grandmama off in mid-sentence and ran from the bedroom into the bathroom, slamming the door behind her. I could hear her gagging. Grandmama followed behind and didn't shut the door.

"When are you gonna tell him?" Grandmama asked.

Mama was silent as she rinsed her mouth at the bathroom sink.

Grandmama shook her head. "Come on." She guided Mama out of the bathroom past me, still behind the potted plant.

I stepped from behind the plant, and followed behind, stopping in the living room and watching as Grandmama sat Mama down at the kitchen table.

Grandmama then busied herself pulling covered bowls and jars from shelves and paper bags from drawers and a wrapped handkerchief from her bosom – pinching a little of this and some of that and mixing everything into a glass of water.

"Here, drink this," she handed the glass to Mama, who made a face, but did as she was told, drinking the murky liquid from the clear glass.

"I know you don't believe in my old-fashioned, old-lady, slavery-time root stuff, like you call it, but when it works, it works. And this works to make all the things you don't want around just…disappear."

Mama stopped drinking out of the glass and stared at Grandmama for a quick second before spitting the liquid from her mouth back into the glass and shoving the glass back at Grandmama.

"Look, Mama. I didn't come here for a lecture or for…" She pointed to the glass, "This. Don't worry about the children; I will take care of my own children. All of them, thank you." Then Mama jumped up from the table and marched out of the kitchen.

"Let's go!" she barked at me, then she slammed through the screen door and into the jungle to find the boys.

I was frozen near the kitchen door. What just happened?

"I don't know," Grandmama shrugged and took a puff from her pipe. Did I say that out loud?

"Well, maybe she don't want *everything* to disappear, just *some* things," Grandmama muttered as she pulled a clear bowl from a shelf over her sink. The bowl was half filled with what looked to be the same murky liquid she tried to get Mama to drink. Something was at the bottom of the bowl. I moved into the kitchen to get a closer look.

At the bottom of the bowl was a bracelet that looked exactly like the one I hated Cousin Nina for admiring on Miss Vera's wrist at the Fourth of July cookout. The same gold, crisscrossed design, with half hearts that joined together at the clasp, to make a whole heart.

"Yeah, Shirley finds all kinda stuff at that motel," Grandmama mumbled on, staring at the bowl.

"You want it?" She turned and shoved the bowl at me. I was now standing next to her at the kitchen sink.

"Nooooo. No, no ma'am," I stammered, backing away from the bowl and the submerged bracelet.

Grandmama shrugged. "Cheap junk anyway. Just trash." With that, she poured the liquid from the bowl into the sink and chucked the bowl and the bracelet into a small garbage pail under her sink.

"Come!" Grandmama turned me around and guided me through the living room and out into the yard.

"Let's go!" Mama yelled at me. She had each boy by the arm

and was trying to drag them out of the yard, but the twins weren't having it.

"Aw! Why, Mama? We want to stay with Grandmama and wait for Granddaddy to come from work."

"The boys can stay," said Grandmama from the doorway. "But take little Miss Nosy here with you." Grandmama gave me a gentle shove down the steps toward Mama. "She's like me. She sees all, so she will keep you honest."

"Thanks, Mama."

"Hmm." Grandmama grunted while puffing her pipe and then took it from her mouth to motion to the twins.

"Come on boys. Grandmama bought some gingersnaps 'cuz I just knew y'all was coming!"

The boys cheered and dashed up the steps, the screen door thwacking behind them.

"Come on! Run!"

Mama yelled at me (again!) and not waiting for me, took off across the overgrown yard and down the sidewalk from West Street onto Logan Street. Up ahead, the King Street-Citadel bus was at the corner of Logan and Beaufain streets. The bus driver was waiting for the light to change. We beat the light and boarded the bus for the rally that Mama had been trying to get to all morning.

12 STAND

The parking lot in front of County Hall was pure mayhem. People were milling everywhere, some with picket signs, some with megaphones exhorting whoever would listen to:

"Get Our Brothers Out of *Nam*!"

"Human Dignity for Our Hospital Workers!"

"Remember Dr. King!"

"Equal Pay for Black Sanitation Workers NOW!"

Forming a ring around this circus, was what looked to be every squad car in the Charleston City Police Department's fleet.

I was scared and wanted to go back to Grandmama's, but Mama marched quickly through the black-and-white squad car brigade, pulling me along with her. We made our way through the crowd until we were at the front doors of County Hall.

"Sorry sister," said a really big man at the door. "It's filled to capacity. Can't let nobody else in."

"But I'm supposed to meet my group here," Mama protested. "My children had to go to the sitter and then the bus and…"

"Sorry, ma'am. It's full. Fire marshal rules. They already lookin' for a reason to throw us outta here, anyway."

"I'm with a Mister Cornell Franklin. He's supposed to be speaking about voting rights. I'm sure if you get him…"

"Lady, I don't know him, I can't leave this door and I can't let you in! Sorry!"

Mama sighed, looking a little lost.

I was overwhelmed by the crowd and the noise. The air was charged with an energy that felt as if things could tip toward chaos at any moment.

"Mama, can we just go home? I just want to go home," I pleaded.

But Mama wasn't listening. "I think that's Cornell speaking now!" She said excitedly.

Loudspeakers at the front of the building were indeed broadcasting the program inside, although no one outside seemed to be paying much attention. We stood for what seemed like forever, Mama transfixed as we listened to Mister Cornell Franklin. He was shouting the last word of every sentence, which brought him some applause, so we only really heard: "Now!" Applause. "Vote!" Applause. "People!" Applause. "Power!" Applause. And finally (thankfully), "Thank you!" More applause.

"Well!" said Mama, now snapped out of her spell.

After Mister Cornell Franklin's speech ended, we drifted aimlessly around the lot, taking in the voter registration tables, picket signs and the impromptu speakers who drew their own small audiences.

Suddenly, the doors of County Hall swung open, and out poured a large group of people. There were reporters moving quickly through the crowd, flash bulbs popping and TV cameras whirring. At the tail end of this entourage was Mister Cornell Franklin, flanked by two ladies who looked like they could be Miss Vera's sisters – big wigs, a jangle of bracelets, tight clothes and all.

Mama saw Mister Cornell Franklin too and plowed her way through the crowd to catch up with him.

"Cornell! Cornell!" She yelled over the din.

Finally, he turned and the two ladies turned with him. The ladies regarded Mama with that same "Who is this thing?" look that Miss Vera gave me and Antoinette when we showed up at the Nugget back in June.

"Cornell! Hi!" Mama was a bit out of breath. "I couldn't get in. I got here late. Too crowded."

"That's all right, sister. It was all good, right ladies?" The ladies nodded in unison but said nothing.

"Listen, we're going over to my mom's to kick back for a few. She's out of town. Why don't you join us?"

"Well, no, I… my daughter's with me and I gotta go pick up my other kids, but I will organize another meeting at my house regarding the sanitation workers and…"

Mister Cornell Franklin cut her off. "Look, about that…we'll talk. We will definitely talk. Look, I gotta go." Mister Cornell Franklin flashed Mama a megawatt smile, about as bright as the flashing cameras around us before he turned and left with his ladies.

Mama again had that lost look, like she did when Miss Vera showed up at the cookout, but only for a second before she yanked me by the hand and dragged me toward the street. Now, she seemed angry. "Let's get outta here. If we hurry, we can catch that bus on its way back around."

She was pulling me so fast that I couldn't keep up. She lost her grip on me, I slipped on some abandoned picket signs and fell hard on my knees to the ground.

The crowd quickly closed at Mama's receding back and before I could figure out whether I should shout for her or cry, the sunlight was blocked by a very tall man with a very big Afro. His mustachioed lips parted into a smile and I was staring at the whitest set of teeth I think I'd ever seen outside of TV.

Without saying a word, he extended his hand and helped me up off the ground. A flash bulb popped. When my vision cleared from the brightness of the flash, the man with the sun-blocking Afro had vanished and the white photographer who took our picture was jogging away.

13 THE NITTY GRITTY

"Girl, you know who that is?" Miss Milly, on a rare daytime visit to the bench because she's always working, was holding the newspaper. Mister and Miss Longs and Mister and Miss Mooney from upstairs, who often made daytime visits to the bench because they don't work anymore, leaned in for a closer look while the kids crowded around.

Mama was standing to one side slightly out of the circle, and so was I, slightly embarrassed to be the center of attention, but not embarrassed enough to stay in the house and miss the commotion.

"That's Mister *Jesse Jackson*! Lawd, he is a good-lookin' man!" exclaimed Miss Milly.

"How'd you get your picture in the paper with him?" A kid asked.

"It's just being at the right place at the right time I guess," said Miss Mooney.

Neither Mama nor I told the unglamorous truth about the events from yesterday that led to my picture being on the front page of the *News & Courier.* Mama, miffed at having been slighted by Mister Cornell Franklin, jerking me through the crowd so hard that I fell down and scraped my knees, and had to be "rescued" off of the pavement by none other than Mister Jesse Jackson himself.

Even though I was clearly sporting scraped knees, no one crowded around the newspaper seemed to notice my injuries. Besides, the way that the photo was shot, it looked like a beatifically smiling Jesse Jackson, taking time out of his busy schedule of helping Black Charleston save itself, bent down to shake hands with an awe-struck girl.

"Did y'all march at the rally right beside him?"

"Yeah, what did y'all sing?"

"Did you get his autograph?"

The questions rained down, but nobody seemed interested in the answers.

"We coulda been in that picture, too, if we ain't stayed at Grandmama's house," said my brother, Peter, who hated seeing me get all that attention.

"Did y'all sing *'Ain't gonna let nobody turn us 'round…?*"

Pat began singing and marching down the sidewalk. Other kids followed along, with the fantasy of Mama and me marching alongside Jesse Jackson overtaking reality. I joined in the play protest too, bored now with the adult conversation that had turned from the beauty of Jesse Jackson to real protests, the strikes and The Man.

"Turn us 'round, turn us 'round. Ain't gonna let nobody turn us 'round. Gonna keep on a'walkin,' keep on a'talkin,' marching on to freedom land!"

With the smell of the garbage that was piling up behind the houses wafting through the air, we sang and marched back and forth, from the corner of Elizabeth and Charlotte to Elizabeth and Henrietta, and back again. On the way back, our voices trailed off, and we were stopped short by a most unusual sight – a blond boy who was standing on the sidewalk next to the Smith house.

"What's wrong with y'all?" someone asked from the bench. "Looks like somebody hit the 'freeze' button."

In silence, we pointed at the yellow-haired boy, who didn't move as he stared at us not moving and staring at him.

The bench emptied of adults, curious at what we were pointing at. We joined the gaggle and continued to stare at the boy, who continued to stare at us.

"Jeremy? We need to…"

A man whose hair was a less blond color than the boy's popped out of the front door of what used to be to Miss Smith's store and joined the boy on the sidewalk.

"Hi. I'm Thomas Smith. This is my son, Jeremy. Good to meet you all." Thomas Smith extended a hand, to no one in particular, but nobody readily extended a hand back, until…

"Hi, I'm Paul." Daddy shook Mister Thomas Smith's hand. "I think we saw you the night of the house fires." Daddy was talking in his white voice again. And where did he come from?

"Yeah, that was me, pajamas and all," Mister Thomas Smith chuckled.

Nobody said anything else, perhaps waiting for Mister Thomas

Smith to explain his presence now and the night of the fire.

As if sensing our unspoken questions, Mister Thomas Smith offered, "I am Adelaide Smith's grandson. The lady who died here recently?"

"Oh's" of understanding from the crowd and a few offers of condolence from the adults.

"Thank you. She was getting on in years. Stubborn old thing, though. Insisted on staying here by herself and running that store. When nobody in the family had heard from her…" his voice trailed off.

So, was he the one who called the ambulance to check on her? Were her cats still in there? Did they make a meal of her, as neighborhood legend now has it? And did he say where he and his son were from?

Again, as if hearing the unspoken questions, Mister Thomas Smith offered, "We live in Philadelphia. I'm into insurance. We're here to collect some of my grandmother's things, sell some of it, if we can, and toss the rest. Say! When is trash pickup? We've got quite a few things that need tossing."

"There is none," someone said.

"Pardon?"

"There's a strike on. The garbage men."

"Oh. That explains the smell."

"I hope you didn't think our neighborhood always smells like this, Mister Smith," said one of the ladies.

"Tom. Just Tom. Oh, no. It's just…noticeable."

Everybody laughed and nodded in agreement.

"We were about to make a run to the dump yard in the North Area if you want to follow behind," Daddy offered, still in his white voice.

We were?

"Cool. I got my trusty VW here." Tom, Just Tom pointed to a blue and white Volkswagen van parked at the curb in front of Miss Smith's house. "Jeremy and I will load up and follow you out." He patted the still-silent Jeremy on the shoulder.

Mister Tom Smith and his son made a move to go back into the Smith house through the store door, but he didn't move fast enough before someone had to ask, because frankly, we all had to know, "So, are you and…Mrs. Smith…thinking about moving in there?"

Mister Tom Smith regarded the house before turning back to the crowd. "I dunno," he said, running his hand through that kind of blond hair. "If I can convince the wife. She's from Pennsylvania. We live just outside Philadelphia. Most of her family's still there. But I wouldn't mind getting away from the hustle and bustle of the big city. Move back South..."

His voice trailed off. As Mister Tom Smith turned and stared wistfully back at the house, the adults nodded politely and shared knowing side glances at each other. Perhaps Mister Cornell Franklin was right with his little speech the other day about, what was that word he used… gentrification?

"So, are y'all taking her cats back with you?" Another adult asked.

"Huh?" The question snapped Mister Tom Smith out of his fantasy of moving back South.

"Her cats?" The adult repeated.

"Cats? We didn't see any cats, did we?" He looked questioningly at his son, who just shrugged. Another round of side glances, this time amongst the kids and adults.

"Cool" Case Study #9

Cool	Not Cool
Having a "root lady" for a Grandmama	Having your Grandmama try to put a "root" on your Mama!
Being a New York City Girl	Having to actually move to New York City to become a New York City girl
Meeting somebody famous like Jesse Jackson	Not really knowing who Jesse Jackson was at the time
Getting my picture in the paper	Having to get my knees scraped up to get my picture in the paper
Summer coming to an end because I'm getting really bored	Having the neighborhood smell like rotting garbage possibly for the rest of the summer
Possibly having a new kid moving into the neighborhood	Having the new kid move into the neighborhood possibly being the end of the neighborhood

14 ONLY THE STRONG SURVIVE

After the trash hauling escapade, the blond Jeremy Smith and his kinda blond dad disappeared as quickly as they had appeared on our sidewalk last week. But the stinky trash piling up in neighborhood backyards remained and hauling garbage to the dump yard up the road had become a weekly event.

In between trips, Mama tried to cover the smell and kill the maggots by pouring Pine-Sol mixed with water over the trash spilling out of two aluminum garbage cans in our backyard. I don't know who told her this would work, because it didn't and in fact made matters worse. The smell was now a gagging mixture of Pine-Sol and rotting garbage, and the maggots seemed to squirm even more.

Daddy was the only person in the neighborhood with a car, so his car became the unofficial trash truck, with the neighborhood men helping to load bags of garbage in the trunk, tying the trunk as closed as it would go with a piece of rope, and riding along to make the drop at the dump.

Correction: Antoinette's dad had a car and a bunch of trucks in his moving business, but I couldn't imagine Mister Brooks, dressed in a suit and tie, hauling garbage. He probably paid people to take their trash away.

"Wanna ride to the dump?" Daddy asked my brothers and me as we stood on the sidewalk, along with the neighborhood kids, watching him and another dad pile bags into the trunk. The boys jumped at the offer.

I was so bored, I said yes, too. I had been avoiding Antoinette since we ran into Miss Vera in the Projects.

"Go tell your mama where you're going," Daddy said to me.

I ran through the screen door, forgetting not to let it thwack loudly behind me, a sound that would normally get Mama to yelling, "You gotta let that screen door slam like that?"

Before the yell could come, I said, "sorry," on my way to the kitchen. The yell never came.

"Mama, we going to the dump with Daddy."

Mama didn't respond. She was sitting at the kitchen table, her Afro squished under a scarf, staring at the TV. Her story was on – *"The Secret Storm."*

"Mama?"

"Hmmm?" She did not turn from the TV.

"Daddy said to tell you we're going to the dump."

"OK. Watch your brothers." She still didn't look up from the TV.

Mama seemed sad lately. What was she sad about? That her

career as Mister Cornell Franklin's sidekick in the fight for jobs, peace and freedom for black Charleston was over before it really began? That her own mama had given her some "root" to drink? That she couldn't figure out how to divorce Daddy and get all of us to New York without him knowing?

Does Daddy even know that she's planning to bolt with us to New York? And if he knows, does he care? Or was she planning to go alone? Will I become like one of the Project Girls – Sherry – who was proud to let everyone know that her mother lived in Newark, New Jersey? I always wondered why she was so proud that her mother didn't live in Charleston with her or that she didn't live in Newark with her mother. Maybe it sounded glamorous to say that her mother lived up North. I don't know if I would like that, no matter how glamorous it might sound to say my mother lives in New York City, without me.

Maybe I should skip the dump, stay home and watch TV with Mama, and watch Mama? If she had a bag packed and stashed somewhere, ready to hightail it to the Greyhound Bus station, she wouldn't leave with me sitting right here. Would she?

"Mama, I think I might stay and…"

Three blasts of the car horn cut me off.

"Watch your brothers," Mama said again, still not looking away from the TV.

Apparently, the dump was the place to be today.

We joined the end of a long queue of cars and trucks, and even a few buses, filled with people and garbage, inching along in the hot sun, waiting our turn to haul our loads atop already giant mounds of garbage in a huge lot. Birds were circling this steaming, stinky mess and I couldn't understand why they didn't just fall from the sky due to the smell. *Can birds smell?*

The boys, who whined loud enough so that Daddy allowed them to sit in the front seat, were wired up by the whole scene and kept bouncing around.

I was in the back seat along with a neighborhood dad, trying not to move at all for fear of A) brushing against the neighborhood dad's very hair legs that were sticking out of makeshift shorts (an old pair of pants cut off at the knees); B) sweating more than I already was; and C) not being able to feel a maggot crawling up on me, should one escape from the trash in the trunk.

Our turn finally came and we hopped out of the car. I hoped that no one was expecting me to help! The boys eagerly grabbed the stinky bags out of the trunk and handed them over to the men, who pitched the bags up on another rapidly growing mound.

A grungy-looking white man who could pass for the brother of the grungy-looking white man who operated the rickety rides at Riverside Beach, was standing by, a cigarette hanging out of his mouth, grumbling, "Hurry up. Hurry up. Hurry it up!"

After the dump adventure, Daddy dropped us off back in the neighborhood and drove away. The neighborhood dad with his homemade shorts and hairy legs, loped off down the street toward the Nugget. The boys joined a kickball game in progress in the yard. The bench was starting to be taken over by the grown-ups, as the long summer day slowly gave way to evening.

Was Mama still in the house or was she halfway to New York by now?

I heard the TV when I entered the living room. That's a good sign, but maybe in her haste to leave town she left the TV on?

Nope. When I got to the kitchen, she was still sitting at the table, now watching *"Dark Shadows."*

"Where are your brothers?" she asked, this time looking away from the TV.

"Outside playing," I answered.

The scarf was gone from her head and her Afro was picked out into a neat halo.

I was glad to see that she hadn't decided to take off for New York without us. So maybe it was safe for me to go over to Antoinette's? Besides, I hadn't seen Antoinette in over a week. Maybe by now she had forgotten about hanging out on the Projects and trying to make friends with the Project Girls.

"Mama, can I go over to Antionette's for a little while?"

"Only for a couple of hours. Then you gotta come back and watch the boys while I'm over at Leah's."

My stomach dropped. Maybe Mama was going to make her escape to New York after all, from Miss Leah's house. Maybe she had a packed bag stashed over there. After all, Miss Leah lived closer to the bus station than we did. Mama could even get there without too many people seeing her, if she went out Miss Leah's back door, crossed

Henrietta Street and cut through the back parking lot of Emanuel Church. She would come out right onto Calhoun Street, between the church and the bus station.

I was frozen in the doorway to the kitchen, again faced with the decision of should I leave or stay and watch TV, and watch Mama?

"You going or not? You running out of time to hang out with Nette." Mama made the decision for me. I was going to Antoinette's house.

I passed the bench and ignored my brothers' "where you going?" I passed the Smith house; a cat was sitting in an upstairs window, looking down at me walking by.

Just before I reached Nette's gate, I had another vision.

Everything went black and I could hear the whistle of a train and feel the ground rumbling under me, like when I stood on the sidewalk outside Mister Henry's store with the box cars swaying inches away. The sound of an oncoming train got louder and the hoot of the whistle more urgent – so much so that I instinctively jumped back, as if I were jumping off of the tracks.

I landed butt first on the sidewalk. The vision cleared but I sat there, huffing and shaking, even though I was in no danger of being run over by a train in front of Antoinette's house. That was the strongest vision that I'd ever had. But as usual, I won't know what it meant until later – like with the bouncing pickle and the red, white and blue cloth flapping in the wind – visions I'd had earlier in the summer.

Before anyone could see me sitting on the sidewalk like a

doofus, I hopped up, made my way down the sidewalk, through the gates and up the porch steps to Antoinette's front door. Before I could ring the bell, the door swung open.

Miss Elmira, the maid.

"Antoinette's at summer camp, baby. She won't be back for another two weeks."

Camp?

Before I could ask any questions, the door swung shut as quickly as it was opened. I was left on the porch trying to process this bit of news. Nette never told me she was going to camp!

Whatever.

Now I was left with nothing else to do. I walked slowly back down the steps and back out onto the sidewalk, contemplating my options.

I could go back home and read old editions of *Weekly Reader*, although I was getting too old to be reading them anymore. Or I could join the kickball game in the yard if it was still going on.

Or I could go over my "Cool Case Study" notes. Was I any closer to being cool in time for school next month? I dunno. I was about to turn thirteen in a few weeks and I still didn't have any ninnies or my period. The only thing that had changed so far was my hair. And to top it all off, whether I was cool or not may not even matter anymore if we were moving to New York City with Mama.

Why were we moving anyway? Because of Daddy and Miss Vera? What exactly *was* the deal with Daddy and Miss Vera, anyway? Maybe nothing. But maybe something, if Grandmama was trying to put root on Miss Vera in an attempt to make her disappear. Did Grandmama's root work? Or was Miss Vera still lingering around, like the trash that was piling up in everybody's backyard?

There was only one way to find out, but did I dare?

I looked back on that day, and the whole summer really, and thought about what I could have, would have or should have done.

I should not have gone into the Nugget back in June with Nette and I would have never known such a lady as Miss Vera existed.

I could have told Mama about the contraband blouse, which she probably would have taken back to the store, and I would not have been able to wear it to Antoinette's party and earn the ire of the Project Girls.

I should not have gone into that closed amusement park by myself and I would not have ended up in the hospital getting stitches and missing the Fourth of July.

I should not have been eavesdropping at doorways, listening to Mama talk to Miss Leah about moving to New York or watching Grandmama trying to put a spell on Mama, and maybe even Miss Vera.

I should have made a right turn from Antoinette's front gate and gone back to the safety of the yard and that kickball game, probably still in progress, or eavesdropped on the gossip at the bench.

But instead, I made a left and…

I guess Grandmama's spell didn't work, because there she was, in the same yard that I saw her in the last time, in the back of her bungalow, standing amongst the strings of clothes lines. She wasn't hanging clothes this time and the dirty kids were nowhere around.

Gone, too, were the dingy housecoat, the head scarf, and the bare face. She was all glammed up this time – sky-high Afro, makeup, hoop earrings, bracelets and bangles galore, even a bracelet high up on one arm. She wore a flowing maxi dress. I wasn't too close, but I thought I could even smell her perfume.

And she was arguing with a man who was arguing back at her.

The man said something Miss Vera must not have liked, because she looked away from him and rolled her eyes to the sky. That's when she noticed me and that's when I noticed the man was...

Daddy!?

She was trying to get him to stop arguing and turn around, but I'm sure I bolted before he did.

Hot-faced, embarrassed, angry and afraid, I ran blindly around the maze that was the Concord Street Projects, turning down one pathway and then another, passing identical dried-mustard-colored bungalows. Wouldn't it be funny if, with all my twisting and turning, I ended up back where I started and ran smack dab into Daddy and Miss Vera, still arguing in her backyard? Not funny, as in "ha, ha," but funny as in how weird stuff like that happens and that would make the day even worse than it already was.

But the day did get even worse, because instead of running into Daddy and Miss Vera, my next turn brought me into the presence of the Project Girls.

"Well, looks like we got a visitor," said Lisa.

Lisa, Rosemarie and Sherry were sitting on the stoop of one of the dried-mustard-colored bungalows, either draped around or draped on by older boys – maybe some of them men? A few of them I recognized from Mister Cornell Franklin's entourage, when he gave the gentrification speech in front of the burnt-out houses. Weren't these guys too old to be hanging out with thirteen-year-old girls?

"Ooooh, fresh meat!" One of the man/boys said, to laughter from the group.

"Come sit a spell. You can sit right here," another one, wearing no shirt, gestured toward his lap.

"Or we can go inside out of this heat and relax in front of the fan while we sip a brew, huh?" Came another, deeper voice.

More laughter from the group, except the Project Girls, who just frowned.

With a quick shrug, Lisa freed herself from under an arm that was draped over her shoulder, with a hand almost grazing her right ninny, jumped off the stoop and put her face inches from mine.

"Where's Rosemarie's blouse, heifer?" Her voice was low and calm.

Sherry jumped off the stoop too, flicking her ponytail as she circled me, adding, "Yeah, where's her blouse? Nobody told you to wear it, heifer. We were gonna come by your house and get it."

They know where I live?

"I still have it," I said quickly.

"She don't really want a blouse you done funked up," Lisa spoke for Rosemarie, who remained silent on the stoop, sitting between the legs of a boy, who yelled out, "Girl fight!"

"Sooo…I guess you gotta get her a new one," said Sherry, still shaking her ponytail, showing off for the boys.

"But I don't have any money," I stammered.

"We don't either," said Sherry. "You know how we shop." She laughed, and so did the other Project Girls.

"I…I can't do that," I said, thinking about the shoplifting scene at Edward's back in June.

"Well, whatcha gonna do?" asked Lisa, still inches from my face. "I want that blouse."

"Hey! I know of a way you can earn some money and buy Rosemarie another blouse," said Sherry.

The girls all looked at each other and chimed as one, "Dugga!"

"Hey, Cornell told you girls to stay outta there for right now until things cool down," cautioned a man/boy from the stoop.

"Man, shut up!" Another man/boy piped in.

"I ain't gettin' in this mess. I'm going inside to cool off with a brew. Y'all coming?" One man/boy rose from the stoop and the others followed.

Rosemarie rose from the step, too, and joined the other girls surrounding me.

"You know Dugga down by the railroad tracks?" Lisa asked.

I nodded yes. "He pays five dollars if you let him touch your ninnies, and I mean under your blouse. He says he'll give you ten dollars if you let him touch your bare boonkey. More, still, if you do some other stuff, but…" Lisa's voice trailed off.

"Yeah, well, we don't do any of that other stuff," said Rosemarie.

"So," says Sherry, "You want to get down with Dugga?"

I was about to say that I couldn't do any of that either, when I thought I heard someone call my name.

Was that Daddy?

"Time's a wasting," said Lisa. "What's it going to be?"

I felt like I was going to throw up, or pee or cry out for Daddy, if that was indeed his voice I'd heard, and if he was indeed looking for me. But was Miss Vera with him, tottering behind in her stack-heeled sandals and clanging bracelets, with that perfume wafting behind her? The thought of having to face her made me want to get out of the Projects as fast as possible, by any means necessary.

"Take me to Dugga," I stared back at Rosemarie.

"Well, okay, then!" Sherry laughed. "Let's go."

Time seemed to have fallen away and the sun seemed to be stuck in the same spot in its summer sky. How long had it been since I'd left the yard, Antoinette's gate, the sight of Daddy and Miss Vera?

Before Daddy (and maybe Miss Vera) could reach me, the Project Girls hustled me along off the Project compound, and onto Concord Street, across an overgrown grassy field, and over to the warehouses and railroad tracks that crisscrossed between them.

The sun beat down on us as we walked down the middle of one of the tracks, the Project Girls expertly skipping along the rail ties, while I stumbled behind. I was afraid that a train would come along and flatten us like the pennies I put on the tracks in front of Mister Henry's store. Was this to be the realization of my train vision?

We seemed to be in an abandoned or little used part of the docks. The warehouses were wooden and rundown looking. We finally stopped in front of one of them, a fading dark green structure that looked as if it would fall down if anyone so much as leaned on it too hard.

"Oh, Dugga, darling, are you in there?" Lisa yelled in a singsong voice toward the big barn-like doors of the building. I looked between the shabby warehouses to the Cooper River sparkling in the sunlight beyond, praying that Dugga was not there.

But God must've been done with my dumb behind, at least for today, and had suspended listening to any of my prayers, because one half of the barn doors to the warehouse creaked open and Dugga peered out, squinting in the bright sunlight.

Dugga looked irritated, as if he were asleep, or doing something else.

"What you little girls want?"

One of the girls pushed me forward.

"We brought you a treat, Dugga. Fresh meat," said Sherry.

"Yeah, how much you got for a little nasty with this one, huh?" Lisa asked.

"She's willing to do whatever you willing to pay for," said Sherry.

Rosemarie was silent.

Dugga's irritation turned to interest. He stepped out of the warehouse, holding a lit hurricane lamp in one hand.

"What's your name, sweet thang?" Dugga shuffled forward, his grin sporting gold on one of the few teeth he had left. I shirked back, but Lisa had me by one arm and Sherry by the other.

"No name, no blame," said Lisa. "Just show us how much you got and we can tell you what all you gonna get."

Dugga reached into a pocket of his dirty coveralls and pulled out a twenty-dollar bill.

"Oooooh," said Sherry at the sight of the money. "Let's see…that'll get you a ninny rub under the blouse, a bare boonkey pat and maybe even a rock up, right, Lisa?"

"Uh huh," Lisa agreed.

I didn't even want to know what a "rock up" was, and how angry was he going to be when he saw that I had no ninnies to rub?

"Bring her in," Dugga said. He retreated through the barn door back into the warehouse. Lisa and Sherry dragged me forward and Rosemarie followed, pulling the warehouse door closed behind her. We were in a cavernous space that smelled of mildew, rotting wood and the salty, swampy smell of the nearby river. I couldn't see much, except Dugga standing too close to me, licking his tongue back and forth along the edge of that gold tooth. He smelled like sweat, liquor, tobacco and God knows what all else.

"Lift your shirt, gal," he whispered hoarsely, holding the hurricane lamp up to my face.

Lisa and Sherry dropped my arms and backed away.

I shut my eyes.

I heard seagulls screaming outside.

I reached for the edges of my blouse.

I heard a train whistle. I slowly pulled up my blouse.

I heard someone shouting.

Was it Daddy? Oh, God, please let it be!

"Dugga!"

That didn't sound like Daddy.

I opened my eyes to the sight of a man walking swiftly toward us, drenched in the shaft of sunlight coming through the now open warehouse door. Behind him were two other people.

Mister Cornell Franklin and two of the man/boys from the stoop.

He pushed Dugga, causing him to stumble backward onto the floor, but still holding onto the hurricane lamp.

"I told you to keep these girls outta here. Look, we gotta work fast. All this stuff's gotta go. Y'all did a real poor job of selling off this stuff. Now, the police are on my butt. Go!"

Mister Cornell Franklin yelled at the two man/boys and pointed to the perimeter of the warehouse, where I noticed for the first time that the walls were lined with dozens of bicycles, open boxes with clothes and shoes piled high. Other closed boxes were stacked all over the place.

"Get outta here!" Mister Cornell Franklin was now yelling at me.

Where were Lisa, Sherry and Rosemarie? When did they leave? And which way was out?

I was disoriented and scared in the giant and dark warehouse, the same way I felt in the murky bar back in June.

I backed toward a wall, watching in what seemed like slow motion, as Mister Cornell Franklin snatched the hurricane lamp from Dugga, who was scampering to stand up off the floor. Mister Cornell Franklin joined the man/boys, who had found other lamps lit around the warehouse, and were tossing them at the bicycles and boxes.

Dugga ran forward in protest. “Stop! Stop! This is my home!”

But he was too late. The fire started quickly.

I felt like I was in a dream as I watched Mister Cornell Franklin trying to tug Dugga away from the flames, eventually giving up when the man/boys tugged Mister Cornell Franklin away, the three of them running off, disappearing into the thickening smoke.

Dugga turned away from the growing flames and ran toward me. I backed away and stumbled down onto a mattress. He reached down and grabbed me by the arm. I screamed and kicked at him. Surely he wasn’t still trying to feel me up in a burning warehouse! He succeeded in pulling me off the mattress and onto the floor and then reached around me to grab a blanket off the mattress.

He ran back toward the flames, trying to put out the fire with the blanket.

I stayed on the floor, still feeling like I was in a dream and studied the little corner I had backed myself into. This indeed appeared to be some sort of home for Dugga. There was a chair and a small wooden table off to one side of the mattress. Near the mattress was a wooden grate, on top of which was a picture of a woman and two children. Who were they? Did Dugga have a wife and kids somewhere?

As I was reaching for the photo, the warehouse doors were flung open.

"Dottie? Dottie!"

Daddy!

Snapped out of my dream state, I rose off of the floor in time to see Dugga run toward Daddy and point in my direction. Daddy ran toward me, lifted me up and ran with me back through the warehouse doors.

I couldn't believe that it was still daylight. I felt like I'd been in the warehouse for hours, first with the Project Girls (where were they now?), and then with Mister Cornell Franklin and the man/boys, (where were they?) and finally, alone with Dugga (where was he?).

Daddy jogged with me in his arms across the railroad tracks and set me down next to…

Mama?

While she was hugging me close, I noticed most of the neighborhood was standing amongst the train tracks, rivulets of water pooling at our feet from nearby fire trucks attempting to put out the flames. When did the fire trucks arrive?

My feet in their worn-down canvas tennis shoes were getting wet. So were the feet of other people standing around – my brothers, wearing canvas sneakers like me; some wearing flip flops tread thin from the long summer; ratty house slippers; cracked work boots; draggers; or just plain bare feet – all getting wet, not noticing or caring as they stared, transfixed by the flames.

I looked up from the wet feet to the faces glowing in the flames, all mostly black like me – my neighbors: Mister Walter and Miss Milly from next door, along with their kids, Ronda, Pat and Darren; the Mooneys and the Longs, and Lucky from upstairs; Miss Leah and her husband Mister Irvin; the Shelton kids; Miss Betty and Sammy and Tommy from down the street; Miss Frannie and her daughter Donnalee from Cedar Court; the men of the corner stores – Mister Costa, Mister Henry, Mister Bongi and Mister Grundgen; even Grandmama and Granddaddy, and the Project Girls.

Right now, the Project Girls, with water pooling around their stolen Hercules sandals, didn't look any cooler than me. They just looked scared, like me.

"Paul, where are you going?" I stopped staring at the faces and turned to look up at Mama, who was looking, horrified at Daddy, as he went back across the tracks.

"Did Dugga come out? I think he's still in there." Daddy quickly surveyed the crowd, looking for Dugga.

"Then tell the firemen!" Mama yelled at his retreating back.

The crowd watched as Daddy went over to the firemen to try to tell them about Dugga and we watched as they shooed him away. And we watched as he gave up on getting them to go into the building to check on Dugga. And we watched as he ran back into the burning building to check for himself.

"Paul!"

Mama screamed, disengaged herself from me and the twins, and tried to run after him. A man in the crowd held her back.

And we were all so transfixed by the fire, the fire trucks, and the firemen and Daddy running back into the burning warehouse and Mama having to be restrained from running after him, that we almost forgot we were standing in the middle of a trainyard…and a train was coming!

"Back up!" A fireman yelled, running toward us.

The crowd took a collective huge step back off the track that the train was hurtling toward us on, that cyclops eye of white light getting closer, its whistle hooting a warning as it drew near.

I was getting goosebumps and that queasy feeling. My vision was coming to life.

The train finally reached us and rushed past, blocking our full view of the burning warehouse. We strained to see between the box cars, getting a full-framed view of the inferno when a boxcar passed that was open on both sides. The whole thing reminded me of those flip cards that my brothers had, whereby a quick flip of the card corners created the illusion of an animated rabbit, jumping out of a black hat, and running away across the cards.

I wished the fire was an illusion, but it was all too real. The smoke. The heat. The sirens. The crowds. The water pooling at our feet.

The train finally passed, just in time for us to get a full view of the warehouse collapsing in on itself.

Someone screamed – or maybe everyone screamed. Or was it just me? I don't know because everything faded to black.

15 LET THE SUNSHINE IN

"Wake up!" One of the twins yelled right into my ear.

But I didn't want to wake up, even though I wasn't really sleeping anymore and had been enjoying the warmth of the sun on my closed eyelids.

I wanted to keep my eyes closed, so that I could savor the dream I just had: I was at my thirteenth birthday party and I was, rightfully, the center of attention. Literally, I was in the middle of the dance floor alone, grooving to Sly and the Family Stone's new tune, *"Hot Fun in the Summertime."*

I was prancing more than dancing, slow walking my way around the circle that was formed by my party guests as they admired my outfit and my hair, which changed each time I came around the circle: Hot pants and sky-high Afro; halter top and bell-bottom jeans, with cornrows; two Afro puffs with a smocked midi top; one Afro bun with a maxi dress.

With each outfit and hair change, the applause from the

admiring crowd grew louder and louder. Everyone was there – Antoinette; my cousins (the ones from Charleston *and* the ones from off), the neighborhood kids, and yes, the Project Girls; even Grandmama and Granddaddy; of course, my brothers, Mama and…

Daddy? Daddy! Where was Daddy?

I opened my eyes in a panic. At the same time, I was scooped up from my resting place.

"You missing all the fun, turkey legs!"

Daddy!

He hadn't called me that in a long time.

He effortlessly jogged with me in his arms across the sand, and into the ocean, then dumped me in.

I squealed because the water felt cold at first, because I really didn't want to get my Afro puffs wet, because it was a bright and beautiful day with blue skies and fluffy white clouds, because we were all together, and because I was happy.

"Not too far, Paul!" Mama yelled from the shore. Her voice seemed tiny as it was swept away by the wind, the roar of the ocean and our screams as my brothers and I took turns with the inner tube, flipping, dipping and diving into the water with Daddy in a day that could go on forever.

But this day wouldn't last forever, and neither would our little family get-away. Tomorrow, we'd load up the car and head away from *Atlantic Beach* and Cabin 10, one of twelve grouped together, and facing the ocean, where we had been staying for the past few nights.

The cabins seemed smaller than two years ago, the last time we stayed at Atlantic Beach. Mama was not happy with the fine dusting of sand on the floor and the occasional ant making its way along the sill of the lone window in the place, but it was nice to get away as a family.

Mama was struggling a bit now as she made her way across the sand, with a blanket and a cooler. She had a plastic tote thrown across her shoulder, packed with our lunch of bologna sandwiches, hard-boiled eggs, fried chicken, tomatoes, and sliced cucumbers and onions that had been marinating in a Mason jar of vinegar, oil, salt and pepper.

Daddy saw Mama and hopped out of the water to help her. At the sight of food, the twins hopped out as well, leaving me alone with the inner tube.

I couldn't swim, but with the inner tube, I felt brave enough to go out far enough for the water to come to my chest, where the beginnings of ninnies were poking out under my swimsuit. Finally!

I turned my back to the beach, and stared off into the watery horizon, enjoying the sound of the waves, the smell of the ocean, the salt in the air, and the wet sand shifting under my feet.

The sun was hot, but the low humidity, the fluffy white clouds and the very blue sky hinted at summer's end.

"Come eat!" Daddy yelled out to me. I turned and waved, but stayed in the water, bobbing around in the inner tube, watching them settle down on the blanket. Mama did too, with a little bit of extra effort. I could see that her stomach was a bit bigger than when the summer began. So, Miss Leah wasn't wrong: There will be four of us sometime in late February, or early March 1970. A new decade, a new brother or sister. News of a new baby was just one of a bunch of things that happened after the warehouse fire, and before our days at the beach…

I had blacked out at the sight of the warehouse collapsing but was revived by Grandmama sticking something really smelly under my nose.

Daddy managed to make his way out of a back door of the warehouse, with Dugga thrown across his shoulder – the same exit Mister Cornell Franklin and the man/boys must have taken when I saw them run deeper into the warehouse, after the fire got going.

After making sure that Dugga got medical attention, Daddy told the police that Mister Cornell Franklin hopped the passing train and made his escape. But the man/boys were caught. I don't know if snitches got stitches back then, but the man/boys spilled the beans. According to what made the news, Mister Cornell Franklin was behind the toy store fire, which he and the man/boys had set to cover for robbing the place, to sell stuff in their misguided attempt to fund the Revolution that Mister Cornell Franklin was planning to wake up sleepy Charleston before the Civil Rights Movement passed us by. The wannabe revolutionary set the abandoned house fires to throw police off the trail of the toy store fire, and of course, he set the warehouse fire to destroy the bikes and other contraband that he had stockpiled there.

As for Dugga, he was an unwitting and unwilling accomplice and he paid for it with his life. He died of smoke inhalation.

The entire neighborhood went to the funeral of Mister Lionel

"Dugga" Duggard. The only family to come to Mister Duggard's funeral was a gaunt-looking half-sister from up North, wearing an ill-fitting wig and accompanied by two sullen children. They were the people I saw in the photo at Dugga's "home." Did anyone in the neighborhood even know that Dugga was living in a warehouse, or was it out of sight, out of mind once he shuffled on by with a tip of his dirty cap?

The funeral was mostly paid for by the owners of the warehouse, who along with the fire and ambulance people, may be in some kind of legal hot water, Daddy said, for paying more attention to putting out the fire than first trying rescue anyone who might have still been in the burning building, and for not immediately offering any medical attention when Daddy emerged with Dugga.

The black *longshoremen* took up a collection for the lone family member of Mister Duggard, which they presented to her during the wake at the little reception hall across the street from our house. The half-sister of Mister Duggard quickly snatched up the offering with a mumbled "thank you," crunching the cash-stuffed envelope deep into her purse.

Daddy made a little speech during the wake about how Mister Duggard's life-ending act of bravery, trying to put out the fire by himself, meant that he will always be remembered for the heroic way in which his life ended, and not how he lived.

And with that statement, which falls under the umbrella of not speaking ill of the dead, I decided not to tell anyone why I was in the warehouse in the first place. Mama just thought I was hanging out with the wrong girls at the wrong time. Daddy thought Rosemarie was my new best friend, because she was the one who told him I was in the warehouse when he ran up, looking for me.

The fact that Daddy was running from having an argument with Miss Vera under her clothesline never came up, either. I know it's different now, but back then, grown-ups didn't feel the need to discuss or explain grown-folk business with their kids, so I'll never know what was going on with Daddy and Miss Vera, and I knew never to ask.

Besides, talk around the bench among the grown-ups was that Miss Vera left her two children with her mama and ran off to New York City with some man who had been in town to promote a concert and who promised to make her a star. Somebody else saw her with said man at a motel up the road. How word of this got back to the bench, I'll never know. When the topic came up one evening while we kids were lurking around, pretending not to listen in, Mama just rubbed her puffy belly and silently sat out making comments on this bit of gossip.

Better Miss Vera goes off to New York than us, anyway. I don't know how I knew that Mama's escape to New York was not going to happen after all, but I knew we weren't going. Maybe it was all talk anyway, but I'm glad that she wasn't talking about it anymore.

"Get out the water!"

That was my entire family yelling at me. How embarrassing. But I got out of the water. Daddy promised he'd take us for ice cream later if no one drowned. I didn't want to be the one to ruin dessert.

The two-hour ride home from Atlantic Beach took us south on U.S. 17, on a long, boring stretch of highway lined with pine trees that made the air smell like somebody spilled a bottle of Pine-Sol in the car.

My brothers were asleep in the back seat next to me. I had to fight for a window seat, which I shouldn't have had to do, because I'm the oldest. Mama and Daddy were up front, quiet, listening to the radio as we rolled down the highway, headed back to Charleston as the night began to gather around us. I let my head hang out of the window a bit, the breeze tossing my Afro puffs, which were a lot less puffy after two days in the ocean. Bug catchers, Mama had called them when she first saw my new hairdo back in June. A bug could fly into my hair right now and I was terrified of bugs, but I was enjoying the breeze, and was even getting used to the strong pine smell.

I was thinking of something Grandmama, and all the grown-ups, really, always said, that trouble comes in threes. Looking over the summer of 1969, I guess they're right.

Let's see...

There were three fires – first, the toy store, then the abandoned houses and, of course, the warehouse.

I had my three visions – the pickle, the red, white and blue cloth, and the train. The pickle vision connected to my three encounters with Miss Vera – at the bar, at the picnic, and in the Projects (four if I counted each Project encounter separately, but I'll count them as one). That leaves my three regrettable encounters with the Project Girls – at Edward's Department Store, at Antoinette's birthday party and in the Concord Street Projects. Does this mean I'll never run into them again? Unfortunately, not. Unless they change schools this fall, there they'll be, Buist School's so-called cool girls, running things like they always did.

Did I still want to be like them? I dunno. I still liked their looks and their confidence. But, besides that, no. Maybe I could work on being cool like *me* this fall. I still had to figure out what *that* meant, though! As for the stupid blouse that started it all, I tossed it in the trash. With all that happened this summer, it didn't seem important anymore. I hoped the Project Girls felt the same way, because if they came at me again about that cheap, old blouse at school, I may have to be like the man/boys snitching on Mister Cornell Franklin and tell all!

We crossed the rickety Cooper River Bridge (which I swear I could feel swaying!), passing the docks and the warehouses, passing the Projects, passing Antoinette's house and the church at the corner where the hospital workers strike began.

Oh, I almost forgot about the strikes! They were over, thank goodness. I guess the hospital workers and the garbage men got what they wanted. I was especially glad that the garbage men were back at work and the squirming trash was gone from everybody's backyard. There were only two strikes, though, so there goes the "bad things in three's" theory, although I guess, the strikes weren't bad things because they didn't devolve into dog-biting, head-bashing, hose-blasting debacles, and both came to a good resolution. Besides, two strikes were probably all that Charleston could handle!

We turned onto Elizabeth Street, past Miss Smith's old house. I almost forgot about her too, dying in that house, all by herself, with just her cats to bear witness. No more sightings of Mister Thomas and son. Did they change their minds about moving to our little town?

The "bad things in three's" saying fell apart here, too. There were only two deaths this summer – Miss Smith and Dugga. I guess if the dying summer was counted, that would be three.

But I wasn't sad the summer was coming to an end, though. I was ready to put the past three months behind me. I was ready to start my last year of middle school; and I was ready to turn thirteen next month. I'd be a real teenager.

How cool is *that*!

"Cool" Case Study #10

Cool	Not Cool
Daddy making that nice speech at Mr. Lionel "Dugga" Duggard's wake	Grandmama, snapping at me at the wake, when I asked her what was that smelly thing she put under my nose after I passed out at the warehouse fire. "Chile, I don't know what you talkin' about! That smoke must've gotten to your head. I was home the whole time with your Granddaddy. I'm too old to be chasing fires!" (Mama confirming Grandmama wasn't there!)
Not moving to New York City and Cousin Nina missing all the excitement because she was in New York City	Me still being pissed that Nina got to go to New York City in the first place
Antoinette getting to go to summer camp	Antoinette pissed because she was at summer camp and missed all the excitement
A new addition coming to the family	Having to cram the new addition into a two- bedroom apartment already bursting at the seams
My 13th birthday coming up next month!	If the Project Girls show up uninvited to my party and start some stuff about that blouse, all over again!
Enjoying a beautiful trip to the beach with my family, but ready to go back to school	Hearing on the radio on the way back from the beach: Black Charleston County school teachers may go on strike!

Extra Cool: Woodstock, a big concert attended by almost a half-million people in upstate New York (August 15-17, 1969).

Not So Cool: It rained a lot, so it looked more like MudFest!!!

GLOSSARY

Angela Davis – A political activist, with a really big Afro!

Atlantic Beach – A historically black beach founded in the 1930s by black business and professional people, because segregation didn't allow blacks on other area beaches.

"Baby, Baby, Don't Cry" – A song by Smokey Robinson and the Miracles.

BC Powder – An aspirin brand.

Blue Laws – Prohibited certain stores from opening on Sundays or, if they were open, they couldn't sell certain things, like toys or beer and wine.

"Bonanza" – A TV western series that debuted in 1955.

Boonkey – Your butt. Not sure of the spelling. To get my boonkey cut meant I was going to get a whipping.

The Bridge – Short for the Cooper River Bridge, which is the less formal name for the two truss bridges that brought traffic into and out of downtown Charleston. To "go across the Bridge" meant you were headed to Mount Pleasant and points around that area.

"Can't Get Next to You" – A song by the Temptations.

Caul – A thin membrane over the face of some newborn babies. Grandmama said that I was born this way and she insisted that it meant that I have psychic abilities. I don't think she's entirely wrong about this.

Charleston Green – A paint color so dark that it looks black but is really green. There's a whole story about how this color came to be… (It involves the Civil War…look it up!)

Chilly bears – Made by pouring Kool Aid into paper cups and sticking the cups in the freezer. Once it was good and frozen, we took them out of the freezer, let them melt for just a bit, (which doesn't take long during a Charleston summer), flipped them over, and put them back into the cup, bottom side up.

Chirren – Children.

"Choice of Colors" – A song by the Impressions.

Conked hair – Chemically straightened hair that was made to "lay down" with some sort of pomade. Whatever pomade my uncle used left a black greasy spot wherever he laid his head!

Coretta Scott King – Wife of slain civil rights leader Dr. Martin Luther King, Jr.

Country – Any place west of the Ashley River. If we're going "out in the country," we were more than likely going to visit relatives on either side of the family, most of whom lived on John's Island. The only other reason to go "out in the country" was to attend a relative's burial at St. James Bethel AME Church Cemetery. (The funeral would most likely be held in the city, if the deceased lived in the city, but everybody got buried "out in the country.") If you described someone as "out the country" or just plain "country," that means they are hopelessly out of fashion – in either speech, manners, dress or all of the above!

"Dark Shadows" – A soap opera about a creepy family that aired from 1966 to 1971. (I think vampires were involved!)

Draggers – Old shoes that could not be worn anywhere else except to "drag" around the house; usually the back of the shoes would be mashed down or cut out to make them into slippers.

Draws – Underwear.

"A Family Affair" – TV series that debuted in 1966 about two sisters and a brother being raised by their uncle and his butler in New

York City.

Fresh – Flirty.

From off – Someone who came to visit town from somewhere else (usually from "up North").

GEX – A store in the *North Area* where we sometimes went for groceries.

Good hair – Reference of the times to black people's hair that was straight, wavy or had a certain type of curl. (I had a lot of hair, but its tight curl and coarse texture was not considered "good.")

The Green – Our unofficial name for Marion Square.

Grown – To act older than your young years.

"Gunsmoke" – A TV western series that debuted in 1955.

"Going in Circles" – A song by the Friends of Distinction.

Hercules sandals – Footwear that borrowed it design from Greek mythology.

"Hogan's Heroes" – TV series that debuted in 1965 which was set in a German prisoner-of-war camp in World War II. (Believe it or not, it was a comedy!)

"Ice Station Zebra" – A spy movie that came out in 1968 and took place in the Arctic.

"It's Your Thing" – A song by the Isley Brothers.

Jesse Jackson – A civil rights activist.

JET magazine – A weekly magazine marketed to African Americans, which featured within its pages the "Beauty of the Week," a swimsuit-clad young black woman.

Kotex – A product for whenever I get my period!

"Let the Sunshine In" – A song by the Fifth Dimension.

Longshoreman – Men who worked the docks, loading and offloading goods from shipping containers, which went to and came from all over the world.

Loose – Act in a manner unbecoming of a young lady.

Magic Eight Ball – A toy shaped like a cue ball that you asked a question of and then shake it to reveal the answer that floats up in a little window in the ball. (Look it up!)

Malcolm X – A civil rights activist.

The Man – White men in power (police, business owners/supervisors, judges, politicians, etc.)

Miss/Mister – "Miss" was used for all women, whether they were married are not, followed by the first name to make it informal, like "Miss Carrie." White women, however, invited no such informality, so they were addressed as "Miss" – again, whether they were married or not – and their *last name*, like "Miss Smith." All men were addressed as Mister and their first name, black or white, like Mister Paul or Mister Thomas. And no adult, woman or man, was called by just their first name by a kid, unless we wanted our boonkeys cut (which means to get a butt whipping)!

The Movement/Civil Rights Movement – Mass protests against racial inequalities.

'Nam – Reference to the Vietnam War (1955-1975).

Nanny roller – The word we used for dung beetles, bugs that like to roll poo-poo. "Nanny" was the word we used for poop. I secretly described my lumpy thick braids as nanny-roller braids because I didn't like them.

The "nasty" – Ummm…partaking in an activity that should be reserved for adults.

Ninny/Ninnies – Breasts.

"The Nitty Gritty" – A song by Gladys Knight & the Pips.

North Area – The part of town north of the city of Charleston before it was incorporated as North Charleston in 1972.

The "numbers" – Unofficial precursor to state-run lotteries.

Octagon soap – A mulit-purpose brand of soap that felt like it had sand in it!

"Oh, What a Night" – A song by the Dells.

"Only the Strong Survive" – A song by Jerry Butler.

Perlo – A rice dish. I learned much later that, regionally, we were actually mispronouncing the word "pilau!"

Piggly Wiggly – A grocery store.

Po' crackers – Poor white people. (Pre-politically correct era!)

Poomp – To fart, pass gas.

Project Girls – My name for a group of girls that lived in a nearby housing project (government-subsidized housing). My name for them wasn't meant to be derogatory. Actually, kids who lived on the projects when I was growing up were considered cool because we saw them as more tough, fearless and free-spirited than we were.

Riverside Beach – Not really a beach, just a gravelly shoreline along the edge of the Cooper River, with a boat landing, some picnic tables and an old pavilion next to a rickety amusement park. It was the most popular of the Charleston area's black beaches in its heyday (before my time), with night clubs attracting entertainers such as Duke

Ellington, Count Basie, Louis Armstrong, B.B. King and James Brown.

Root woman – Someone who believed in using herbs and other items (like animal bones) to "see" futures, heal illnesses and maybe "fix" people or situations, like with a spell. (My Grandmama on my mother's side was considered a root woman.)

"Rosemary's Baby" – Horror movie that came out in 1966 starring Mia Farrow.

"Runaway Child, Running Wild" – A song by the Temptations.

"Secret Storm" – A soap opera (1954-1974), one of several of Mama's "stories," as she called them. We knew to leave her alone when her "stories" were on.

Skeetah Beach – The informal name of "Mosquito Beach," a local black hangout for adults consisting of a collection of party shacks on the edge of swampland off the Atlantic Ocean. This beach was aptly named for the swarm of the blood-sucking bugs that latched on to any exposed flesh the minute you stepped out of the car.

A slip – An undergarment worn under a dress. (They were falling out of fashion by the 1960s as the styles were changing, which was probably why I was wearing them by then as pajamas. I don't think they even exist anymore!)

Southern Christian Leadership Conference – Established in 1957 to coordinate the action of local protest groups throughout the South.

"Stand" – A song by Sly and the Family Stone.
"Star Trek" – A sci-fi TV series that first aired in 1966.

To switch – To sway your hips and butt from side to side in an exaggerated manner as you walk (to attract attention from boys/men).

Teejun – The word is really "artesian," as in water from an artesian well, but everybody just said "tee-jun." There was a fountain on the *Green* that mostly old people went to – black and white – with jugs and bottles in hand, to get some of that teejun water, which was said to have curative value. (I didn't like it because I thought that water smelled too "natural," tasted "green" and felt slimy on my teeth and tongue).

Tell a story – To tell a lie. (My parents didn't like for us to use the word "lie" as kids!)

"Think" – A song by Aretha Franklin

"Time is Tight" – A song by Booker T & the MGs.

Touched – Slightly off in the head, mentally unbalanced. (Again, pre-politically correct era!)

Up North – Any state above Maryland (such as Pennsylvania, New Jersey, New York, etc.)

Up the road – You're headed to the *North Area* of the city.

"Walk on By" – A song by Isaac Hayes.

Weekly Reader – A weekly magazine for students, in circulation from 1928 to 2012.

"What Does It Take" – A song by Jr. Walker & the All-Stars.

ABOUT THE AUTHOR

Dorothy Givens Terry is a native of Charleston, South Carolina. She graduated from Howard University's School of Communications with a bachelor's degree in Print Journalism, and from Georgetown University with a master's degree in Public Relations and Corporate Communications.

She has written professionally as a reporter for the *Post & Courier* newspaper in Charleston and the *San Diego Union Tribune.* She has also written as a freelance journalist for magazines and journals and was once a Capitol Hill press secretary.

She is a proud member of Alpha Kappa Alpha Sorority, Inc., and a founding member of the South Carolina Coastal Association of Black Journalists of the National Association of Black Journalists.

www.ingramcontent.com/pod-product-compliance
Lightning Source LLC
LaVergne TN
LVHW091311150826
845673LV00006B/1613

9798218273316